Asterix Omnibus 9

ASTERIX AND THE GREAT DIVIDE,
ASTERIX AND THE BLACK GOLD,
ASTERIX AND SON

Written and illustrated by ALBERT UDERZO

Orion
Children's Books

ORION CHILDREN'S BOOKS

ASTERIX®-OBELIX®
Exclusive licensee: Hachette Children's Group
Translators: Anthea Bell and Derek Hockridge
Typography: Bryony Newhouse

First Published in Great Britain in 2014 by Orion Children's Books Ltd
Paperback edition first published in Great Britain in 2015 by
Orion Children's Books Ltd
This edition published in 2016 by Hodder and Stoughton

3 5 7 9 10 8 6 4

A CIP catalogue record for this book is available from the British Library

ISBN 978 1 4440 0967 5 (cased)
ISBN 978 1 4440 0966 8 (paperback)

Printed in China
The paper and board used in this book are from well-managed forests and other responsible sources.

Orion Children's Books
An imprint of Hachette Children's Group, part of Hodder and Stoughton
Carmelite House, 50 Victoria Embankment
London EC4Y 0DZ
An Hachette UK Company

www.hachette.co.uk
www.asterix.com
www.hachettechildrens.co.uk

THE YEAR IS 50 BC. GAUL IS ENTIRELY OCCUPIED BY THE ROMANS. WELL, NOT ENTIRELY ... ONE SMALL VILLAGE OF INDOMITABLE GAULS STILL HOLDS OUT AGAINST THE INVADERS. AND LIFE IS NOT EASY FOR THE ROMAN LEGIONARIES WHO GARRISON THE FORTIFIED CAMPS OF TOTORUM, AQUARIUM, LAUDANUM AND COMPENDIUM ...

ASTERIX, THE HERO OF THESE ADVENTURES. A SHREWD, CUNNING LITTLE WARRIOR, ALL PERILOUS MISSIONS ARE IMMEDIATELY ENTRUSTED TO HIM. ASTERIX GETS HIS SUPERHUMAN STRENGTH FROM THE MAGIC POTION BREWED BY THE DRUID GETAFIX . . .

OBELIX, ASTERIX'S INSEPARABLE FRIEND. A MENHIR DELIVERY MAN BY TRADE, ADDICTED TO WILD BOAR. OBELIX IS ALWAYS READY TO DROP EVERYTHING AND GO OFF ON A NEW ADVENTURE WITH ASTERIX – SO LONG AS THERE'S WILD BOAR TO EAT, AND PLENTY OF FIGHTING. HIS CONSTANT COMPANION IS DOGMATIX, THE ONLY KNOWN CANINE ECOLOGIST, WHO HOWLS WITH DESPAIR WHEN A TREE IS CUT DOWN.

GETAFIX, THE VENERABLE VILLAGE DRUID, GATHERS MISTLETOE AND BREWS MAGIC POTIONS. HIS SPECIALITY IS THE POTION WHICH GIVES THE DRINKER SUPERHUMAN STRENGTH. BUT GETAFIX ALSO HAS OTHER RECIPES UP HIS SLEEVE . . .

CACOFONIX, THE BARD. OPINION IS DIVIDED AS TO HIS MUSICAL GIFTS. CACOFONIX THINKS HE'S A GENIUS. EVERYONE ELSE THINKS HE'S UNSPEAKABLE. BUT SO LONG AS HE DOESN'T SPEAK, LET ALONE SING, EVERYBODY LIKES HIM . . .

FINALLY, VITALSTATISTIX, THE CHIEF OF THE TRIBE. MAJESTIC, BRAVE AND HOT-TEMPERED, THE OLD WARRIOR IS RESPECTED BY HIS MEN AND FEARED BY HIS ENEMIES. VITALSTATISTIX HIMSELF HAS ONLY ONE FEAR, HE IS AFRAID THE SKY MAY FALL ON HIS HEAD TOMORROW. BUT AS HE ALWAYS SAYS, TOMORROW NEVER COMES.

R. GOSCINNY Asterix A. UDERZO
Asterix
AND THE GREAT DIVIDE
Written and illustrated by Albert UDERZO
UDERZO

GOSCINNY AND UDERZO

PRESENT

An Asterix Adventure

ASTERIX AND THE GREAT DIVIDE

Written and Illustrated by ALBERT UDERZO

Translated by Anthea Bell *and* Derek Hockridge

Orion
Children's Books

SOMEWHERE IN GAUL, PEACE WOULD BE REIGNING IN A LITTLE VILLAGE VERY LIKE THE VILLAGE WHERE ASTERIX LIVES...

...BUT FOR VARIOUS PECULIAR INCIDENTS. A BIG DITCH HAS BEEN DUG THROUGH THE MIDDLE OF THE VILLAGE, SO THAT NO ONE CAN GET FROM THE RIGHT SIDE TO THE LEFT SIDE.

CLEVERDIX HAS BEEN ELECTED CHIEF BY THE LEFT OF THE VILLAGE...
NEVER MIND WHAT THE OTHER LOT SAY, I'VE BEEN UNANIMOUSLY ELECTED VILLAGE CHIEF!

MAJESTIX HAS BEEN ELECTED CHIEF BY THE RIGHT OF THE VILLAGE... MONARCH OF HALF HE SURVEYS.
BY DIVINE RIGHT!

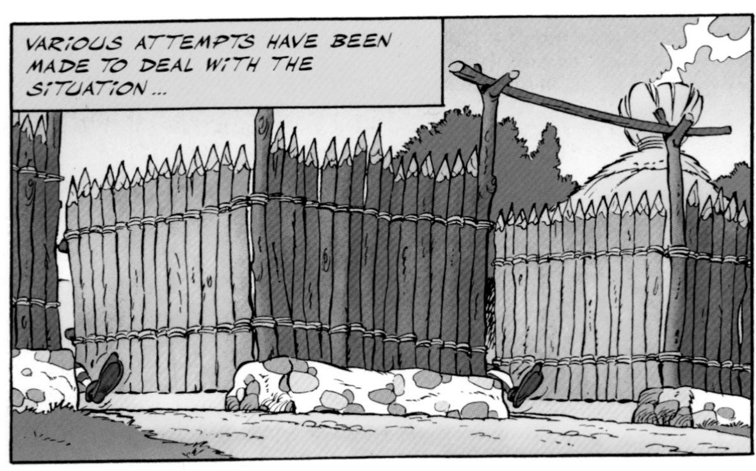
VARIOUS ATTEMPTS HAVE BEEN MADE TO DEAL WITH THE SITUATION ...

AND THE VILLAGERS OF THE LEFT AND THE RIGHT ARE EVER READY TO EXPRESS THEIR MUTUAL ANTAGONISM.
RSPRR!
RSPRRR!

BUT IT WOULD TAKE POSITIVELY SINISTER DEXTERITY TO SOLVE CERTAIN VITAL PROBLEMS ...
?!
?!

... AND ONLY THE CHILDREN ARE ANY BETTER OFF FOR THE RIFT.
SCRUNCH
YOU'VE GOT NO RIGHT TO DO THAT! THAT'S MY TREE!!!

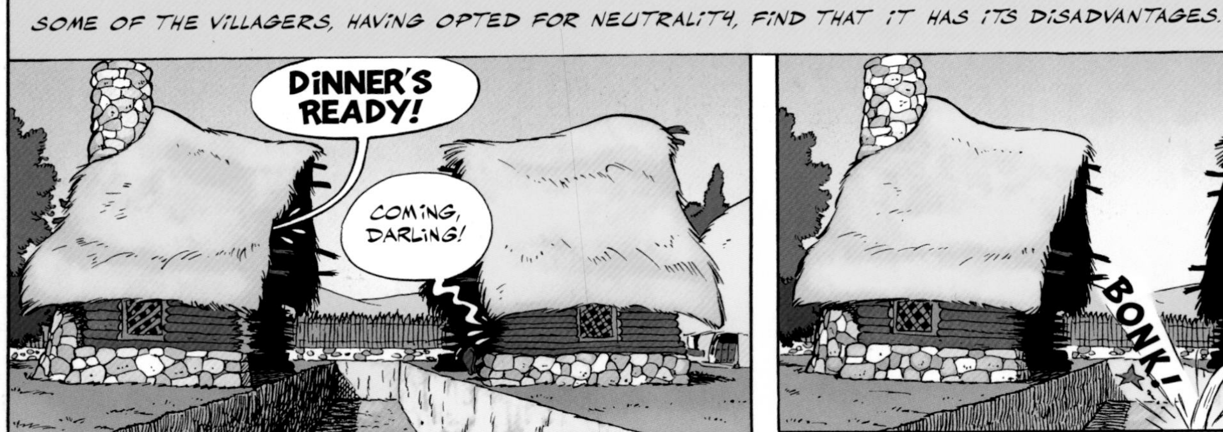
SOME OF THE VILLAGERS, HAVING OPTED FOR NEUTRALITY, FIND THAT IT HAS ITS DISADVANTAGES.
DINNER'S READY!
COMING, DARLING!

BONK!

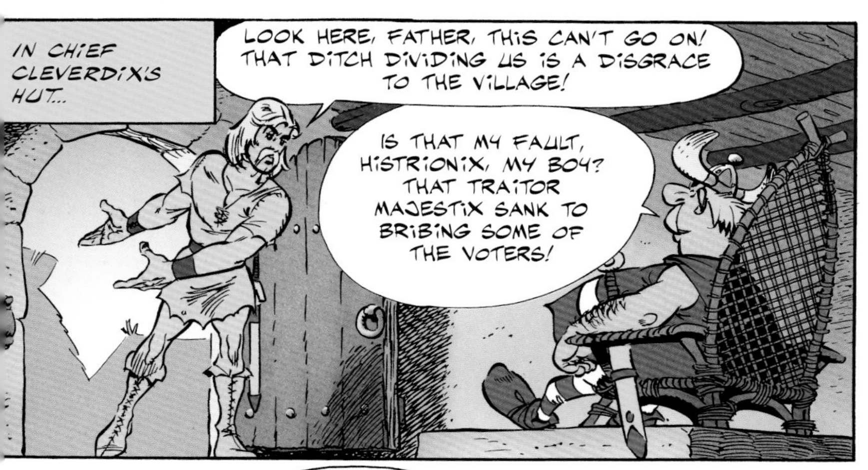

IN CHIEF CLEVERDIX'S HUT...
LOOK HERE, FATHER, THIS CAN'T GO ON! THAT DITCH DIVIDING US IS A DISGRACE TO THE VILLAGE!
IS THAT MY FAULT, HISTRIONIX, MY BOY? THAT TRAITOR MAJESTIX SANK TO BRIBING SOME OF THE VOTERS!

HE AND HIS HENCHMAN, THE UNSPEAKABLE CODFIX, HAD THE NERVE TO GET VOTES FROM VILLAGERS WHO WERE ONLY BABES IN ARMS!

WELL, AT THIS RATE FUTURE GENERATIONS OF GAULS AREN'T GOING TO THINK MUCH OF THEIR ANCESTORS!

CAN YOU SUGGEST ANYTHING, FATHER?
YES, MY BOY, I CAN. I'VE DECIDED TO MAKE A SPEECH TO THE VILLAGERS OPPOSITE. THAT'LL BRIDGE THE GAP. THEY'LL SOON SEE HOW WRONG THEY WERE TO DITCH ME!

AND IN CHIEF MAJESTIX'S HUT...
OH, FATHER, DO YOU REMEMBER HOW HAPPY THE VILLAGE WAS WHEN WE ONLY HAD ONE CHIEF, ALTRUISTIX?
YES, I DO! THE OLD SO-AND-SO TOOK AFTER HIS COUSIN ALCAPONIX... MAKING OFF WITH ALL THE VILLAGE'S TAXES!

THIS IS ALL THAT FOOL CLEVERDIX'S FAULT! HE STOLE VOTES WHICH WERE MINE BY RIGHT.

HE EVEN PROMISED TO BRING DOWN INFLATION, AND THOSE IDIOTS FELL FOR IT! THAT WAS WHEN THE BALLOON WENT UP!

MELODRAMA IS RIGHT! WE NEED A SINGLE CHIEF TO LEAD THE VILLAGE. YOU LET THEM KNOW OVER ON THE LEFT THAT YOU'RE THE RIGHTFUL CHIEF!
CODFIX, YOUR ADVICE ISN'T ALWAYS CODSWALLOP! YES, I'LL ADDRESS THEM!

AND SOON AFTERWARDS...

BROTHERS, WE ARE HOVERING ON THE BRINK OF VILLAGE DISASTER! BUT THE PARTY OF THE LEFT OFFERS FULL EMPLOYMENT... MAXIMUM PRODUCTIVE POTENTIAL FOR ALL WORKERS...
...SHIELDBEARERS INCLUDED. DON'T YOU LISTEN TO MAJESTIX! HE'D PLUCK THE VERY WINGS FROM YOUR HELMETS! WORKERS OF THE VILLAGE, UNITE!

CROSS THE GREAT DIVIDE!
SPLATCH!

POPULAR OPINION HAS REPLIED IN THE ONLY FITTING WAY TO THE LYING INSINUATIONS OF THAT DOUBLE-DEALING CLEVERDIX! WITH HIS BRINKMANSHIP, HE'D HAPPILY SACRIFICE THE GOOD OF THE VILLAGE TO THE INTERESTS OF ROME, SPOUTING HOT AIR ON BEHALF OF THE ROMAN GEEZER*...
FRIENDS, GAULS, COUNTRYMEN, LET US THROW IN OUR LOT TOGETHER!
* JULIUS CAESAR

COME TO MY...
SPLATCH!

VERY WELL, LET'S FIGHT IT OUT, YOU ROTTEN LOT, AND WE'LL SEE WHO'S LEFT IN COMMAND!
BY ALL MEANS, AND WE'LL SEE YOU DO A RIGHT ABOUT TURN!

RSPRRRRR!
RSPRRRR!

COME ON, LADS! I'M RELYING ON YOU TO SHOW 'EM THE PARTY OF THE LEFT IS IN THE RIGHT OF IT!
COME ON MEN! LET 'EM SEE THE PARTY OF THE RIGHT ISN'T GOING TO BE LEFT AT THE POST!
SOON AFTERWARDS...
WELL DONE, LADS! WE SET THEM RIGHT ALL RIGHT! LET'S GO HOME NOW!
WELL DONE, MEN! YOU LEFT THEM STANDING ON THE LEFT! LET'S GO HOME NOW!
RSPRRRRR!
RSPRRRRR!
RSPRRRRR!

ELSEWHERE, PEACE IS REIGNING IN ANOTHER LITTLE VILLAGE, A VILLAGE WE ALL KNOW WELL...

LOOK, IF PEACE IS REIGNING IN OUR LITTLE VILLAGE, THE VILLAGE THEY ALL KNOW WELL, THAT MEANS THE ROMANS ARE SULKING, ASTERIX!
NO, OBELIX, IT JUST MEANS THEY'VE LEARNT A BIT OF SENSE!

?!

WHAT ARE YOU DOING ON THAT CONTRAPTION, O CHIEF VITALSTATISTIX?
ER... WELL... I'M GOING OUT SHOPPING FOR IMPEDIMENTA. SHE'S FEELING A BIT UNDER THE WEATHER.

BUT WHAT'S THE CART FOR?
OH, THE CART! THAT'S A NEW IDEA OF MINE. IT MEANS THESE CLUMSY GREAT OAFS CAN'T LET ME DOWN ANY MORE WHEN THE FANCY TAKES THEM.

RIGHT, YOU TWO! WHATEVER YOU DO NOW, I STAND FIRM ON MY TRUSTY SHIELD! SO OFF WE GO SHOPPING!

!
BONG!

SIGH
AND HE CAN'T SHOP US FOR THAT, OR GET NEW SHIELDBEARERS...
NO, WE SHIELD-BEARERS OPERATE A CLOSED SHOP!

DOWNCAST AGAIN, PIGGYWIGGY? THINKING YOURSELF SO CLEVER... HUH! PIGS MIGHT FLY!

GENIX
FISHMONGER
Seafood
BY BELENOS, SO YOU'RE STILL THE FALL GUY, CHIEF VITALSTATISTIX?
SHUT UP AND SERVE ME! AND FAST! YOU COULD CUT THE ATMOSPHERE AROUND HERE WITH A KNIFE!

AND JUST WHAT DO YOU MEAN BY THAT?
I MEAN YOU GET A THUMP UP THE HOOTER IF YOU DON'T HURRY UP, THAT'S WHAT!!

NOW, LADDIE, THE THING IS TO STRIKE WHILE THE IRON IS...
BIFF!
BANG! BANG!

...HOT...
SPLATCH!

AND HERE'S A STRIKING EXAMPLE OF ACTING IN THE HEAT OF THE MOMENT!
!
BIFF! BANG!
7A

PLATCH!

GERIATRIX, SWEETIE-PIE, DON'T GO FAR! DINNER'S NEARLY READY!
JUST TAKING SOME EXERCISE TO WORK UP AN APPETITE!

THESE GAULS ARE CRAZY!
TAP! TAP! TAP!
BIFF! BING! BANG!

SPLOTCH!

I CAN'T KEEP A FISH WHICH DOESN'T BELONG TO ME, CAN I, ASTERIX? I'LL RETURN IT TO THE OWNER WHILE YOU GET DINNER!
7B

Fish
UNHYGIENIX
FISHMONGER
Seafood

DINNER'S READY!
DINNER'S READY!
DINNER'S READY!
DINNER'S READY!
DINNER'S READY!
DINNER'S READY!
DINNER'S READY!
Fish
UNHYGIENIX
FISHMONGER

LISTEN, WHY DON'T WE CARRY ON LATER TO HELP OUR DINNER DOWN?
AND MEANWHILE, WOULD YOU MIND HELPING ME DOWN? MY WIFE'S WAITING!

THESE FISH ARE ALMOST PAST IT, EVEN FOR HELPING PEOPLE RELAX. CHANGE AND DECAY IN ALL AROUND I SEE...

MEANWHILE...
AND JUST WHAT GOOD DID THAT PUNCH-UP DO YOU? ABSOLUTELY NONE! IT ONLY WIDENED THE RIFT BETWEEN THE PEOPLE OF OUR VILLAGE!
YOU DON'T UNDERSTAND THE FIRST THING ABOUT POLITICS AND THE ART OF WARFARE, MY GIRL! GO UP TO YOUR ROOM AND LEAVE US ALONE!

HEAR THAT? SHE'LL SOON BE JOINING CLASSICAL WOMEN'S LIB, SPEAKING TO THEM OFF THE CUFF*!
ALL THE SAME, YOU HAVE TO ADMIT THAT TODAY'S LITTLE CONFRONTATION DIDN'T GET US ANYWHERE.
*LATIN: AD LIB

I KNOW. I JUST CAN'T SEE WHAT TO DO NEXT!
WELL, O CHIEF MAJESTIX, I'D LIKE TO MAKE YOU AN OFFER!

GIVE ME MELODRAMA'S HAND IN MARRIAGE, AND I WILL COME UP WITH THE ANSWER TO ALL YOUR PROBLEMS!
OH YES? AND WHAT'S THAT?

THE ROMAN ARMY!
?!?

DON'T YOU THINK YOU'RE GOING A BIT FAR, CODFIX? ROMANS!!! FOR A START, WHY WOULD THEY COME TO MY AID OVER OUR SPOT OF TROUBLE HERE?
I CAN BRING INFLUENCE TO BEAR ON THE GARRISON OF THE NEAREST FORTIFIED CAMP. LEAVE IT ALL TO ME! SOON YOU'LL BE CHIEF OF THE WHOLE VILLAGE!

I'M STILL NOT KEEN ON HAVING FOREIGNERS MIXED UP IN OUR AFFAIRS. ESPECIALLY ROMANS. PAX ROMANA OR NO PAX ROMANA, THEY'RE OUR ENEMIES!
HAVE NO FEAR! AS SOON AS THE TROUBLE'S CLEARED UP, THEY'LL GO PEACEFULLY BACK TO THEIR OWN CAMP!

RIGHT! IT'S A DEAL CODFIX! I PUT MYSELF IN YOUR HANDS, BUT YOU'RE NOT MARRYING MELODRAMA UNTIL I'M THE ONLY CHIEF IN THE VILLAGE... CHIEF OF THE LEFT AS WELL AS THE RIGHT!
CONSIDER YOURSELF CHIEF, DAD, AND CONSIDER ME MR RIGHT!
SHAKE!

A WELL BROUGHT-UP GIRL DOES NOT LISTEN THROUGH FLOORBOARDS!
MAYBE NOT, BUT A GIRL WITH ANY SENSE DOES!

ANGELICA, MY DEAR OLD NURSE, I WANT YOU TO GO AND SEE HISTRIONIX AND TELL HIM THERE'S SOMETHING SERIOUS AFOOT. ASK HIM TO MEET ME ON MY BALCONY TONIGHT! AND HURRY!

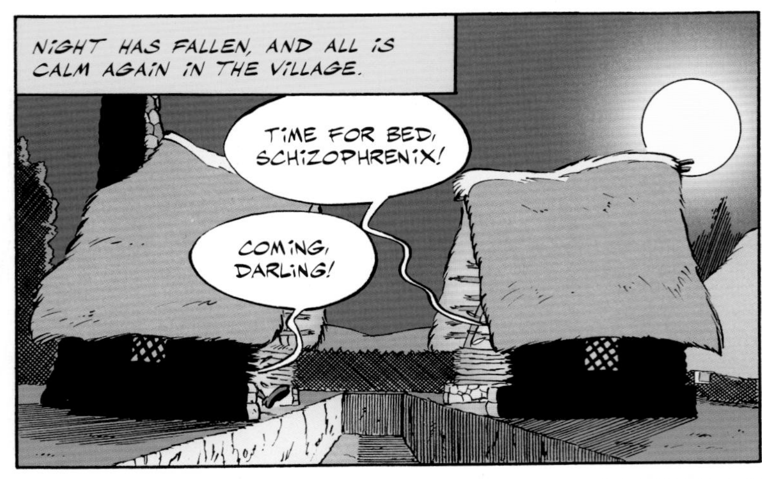
NIGHT HAS FALLEN, AND ALL IS CALM AGAIN IN THE VILLAGE.
TIME FOR BED, SCHIZOPHRENIX!
COMING, DARLING!

BONG!

CODFIX IS GOING TO ASK THE ROMANS TO HELP MAKE MY FATHER CHIEF OF THE WHOLE VILLAGE... AND IN RETURN MY FATHER HAS PROMISED HIM MY HAND IN MARRIAGE!

HOW DARE HE?! BUT I'M FROM THE OPPOSITE CAMP, MELODRAMA... WHY ARE YOU TELLING ME ALL THIS?
BECAUSE YOU'RE THE ONLY PERSON WITH ANY SENSE IN THIS CRAZY VILLAGE, AND I DON'T WANT TO MARRY CODFIX! O HISTRIONIX, HISTRIONIX! WHEREFORE ART THOU HISTRIONIX?
?

!?!

RAISE THE ALARM!

BONK!

ARE YOU HURT, HISTRIONIX?
NO, I'M ALL RIGHT... I FANCY A PASSING SHOAL OF FISH BROKE MY FALL!

MY OWN DAUGHTER IN LEAGUE WITH THE ENEMY! TREACHERY UNDER MY OWN ROOF!
AND MY OWN FATHER ISN'T ASHAMED TO ASK THE ROMANS FOR HELP IN FIGHTING OUR OWN FRIENDS AND RELATIONS!

SHUT UP, YOU UNGRATEFUL CHILD! I'M GOING TO LOCK YOU IN YOUR ROOM, AND YOU DON'T COME OUT UNTIL THE DAY YOU MARRY CODFIX!
I NEVER WILL! I'D RATHER BE A VIRGIN SERVING VESTA* ALL MY LIFE!
*GIRLS CURRIED FAVOUR WITH THIS GODDESS

DON'T LET'S RUSH THIS MAJESTIX! TIME AND PATIENCE WILL ACHIEVE MORE THAN RAGE AND VIOLENCE EVER COULD!
GNGNGNGNGNGN!

SOMETIMES I WONDER HOW I THINK THESE THINGS UP...

O LOVELY MELODRAMA, PLEASE ACCEPT THIS PRETTY BUNCH OF FLOWERS!

WHAT MAKES YOU THINK YOU'RE A SMASH HIT WITH ME?
BANG!

MEANWHILE...
FATHER, WAKE UP!
HMPH? WHAT IS IT?

MAJESTIX AND HIS HENCHMAN CODFIX ARE PLANNING TO ASK THE ROMANS TO HELP THEM CONQUER THE WHOLE VILLAGE!
OH, ARE THEY? WELL, SON, I WANT YOU TO GO IN SEARCH OF MY OLD COMRADE-IN-ARMS VITALSTATISTIX. HE AND I FOUGHT TOGETHER AT GERGOVIA...

HE'S CHIEF OF AN ARMORICAN VILLAGE A FEW DAYS' JOURNEY AWAY. THANKS TO THE DRUID GETAFIX'S MAGIC POTION, HE HAS KEPT THE WHOLE MIGHT OF CAESAR'S LEGIONS AT BAY! EXPLAIN IT ALL TO HIM, AND TELL HIM I NEED HIS HELP!

A FEW DAYS LATER...
HOW I ENVY THE PEOPLE OF THIS VILLAGE! LIVING IN SUCH PERFECT PEACE AND HARMONY...

SPLATCH

YOU STUPID IGNORANT LOT! I'M NOT SELLING ANY MORE OF MY FISH TO THOSE WHO DON'T APPRECIATE ITS TRUE WORTH!
GOOD!!! THOSE WHO APPRECIATE ITS TRUE WORTH WILL TURN IT INTO GLUE, AND IT WON'T SMELL SO BAD!!!
?!

IF THIS CARRIES ON MUCH LONGER, ASTERIX, THEY'LL BE DISCOVERING NUCLEAR FISHION!
AHEM!

CAN YOU TELL ME WHERE TO FIND VITALSTATISTIX, CHIEF OF THIS VILLAGE?
?

VITALSTATISTIX? HE'S ON HIS WAY!

STOP! AND THAT'S AN ORDER!

SCR EE.CH

I'M GOING TO CRACK UP ... I CAN FEEL IT COMING ON! YES... I'M GOING TO CRACK UP ...

THIS IS IT! I'M CRACKING UP!

...AND THAT, O CHIEF VITALSTATISTIX, IS THE SAD STORY OF OUR VILLAGE. ONLY YOUR DRUID GETAFIX'S MAGIC POTION AND THE WISDOM OF YOUR EXPERIENCED WARRIORS CAN SAVE US!
HMPH, YES. SPEAKING OF THE WISDOM OF MY EXPERIENCED WARRIORS, I SOMEHOW FEEL I SHOULD BE PUTTING MY OWN HOUSE IN ORDER FIRST...

...BUT SINCE THE ROMANS LOOK LIKE GETTING MIXED UP IN YOUR AFFAIRS, I DON'T SEE WHY I SHOULDN'T LEND MY OLD COMRADE-IN-ARMS CLEVERDIX A HAND!

THANK YOU... AND ON MY OWN BEHALF TOO! UNLESS WE FIND A PEACEFUL SOLUTION, MELODRAMA AND I CAN NEVER HOPE TO BE UNITED!

BOOHOOHOOO
?

BOOHOOHOOHOO

WHAT'S THE MATTER, OBELIX?
SNIFF! I GET ALL UPSET BY LOVE STORIES WITH UNHAPPY ENDINGS! SNIFF!
HUH!

BUT THIS STORY'S ONLY JUST BEGINNING, AND IF CHIEF VITALSTATISTIX WILL LET US, WE'RE GOING TO HELP HISTRIONIX SOLVE HIS PROBLEMS!
OOH, YES, LET'S! GOODY, GOODY, GOODY!
WOOF! WOOF!

THE ROMANS AROUND HERE ARE KEEPING VERY QUIET JUST NOW, SO I THINK I CAN JOIN THE EXPEDITION MYSELF! THE PEOPLE OF YOUR VILLAGE MAY NEED ME TO HELP THEM BRIDGE THE GREAT DIVIDE!

ND A LITTLE ATER...
WILL HE SING? WON'T HE SING? WILL HE SING? WON'T HE SING?

IN THE ROMAN CAMP NEAR THE DIVIDED VILLAGE...
HEY, SOURPUS, I'LL SWAP YOU TWO SENTRY DUTIES FOR ONE LAUNDRY FATIGUE!
NOTHING DOING! YOU ALREADY OWE ME THREE COOKHOUSE FATIGUES AND TWO LATRINE FATIGUES!

BACK AT THE RECRUITMENT OFFICE, THEY TOLD US WE'D GET BEAUTIFUL SLAVE-GIRLS FROM THE COUNTRIES WE CONQUERED...
BACK IN ROME, CAESAR SAID HE WAS COUNTING ON US TO CLEAN UP THE BARBARIANS... WHAT A WASH-OUT!
LOOT, THEY SAID. THE CARROT FOR THE DONKEY!
IT'S A MAN'S LIFE IN THE ARMY, THEY SAID...
ALL RIGHT, WE KNOW, WE KNOW!

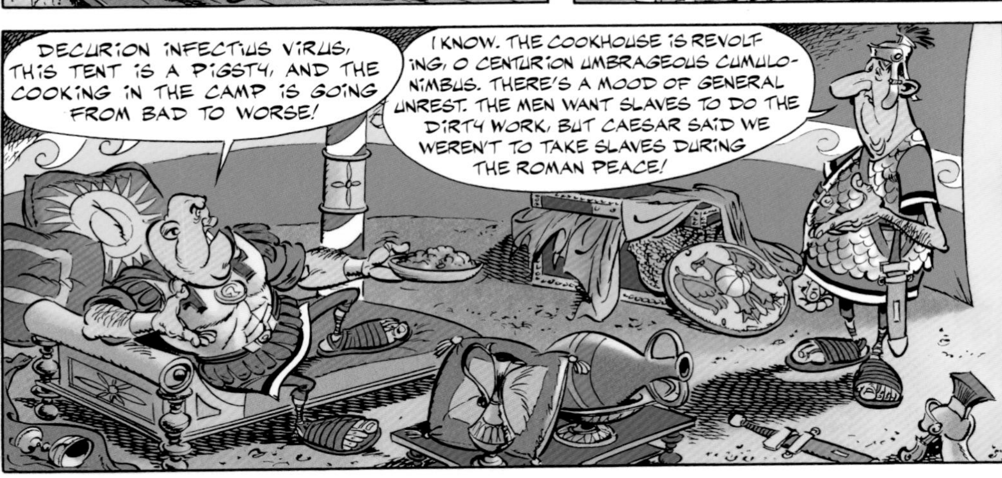
DECURION INFECTIUS VIRUS, THIS TENT IS A PIGSTY, AND THE COOKING IN THE CAMP IS GOING FROM BAD TO WORSE!
I KNOW. THE COOKHOUSE IS REVOLTING, O CENTURION UMBRAGEOUS CUMULONIMBUS. THERE'S A MOOD OF GENERAL UNREST. THE MEN WANT SLAVES TO DO THE DIRTY WORK, BUT CAESAR SAID WE WEREN'T TO TAKE SLAVES DURING THE ROMAN PEACE!

WISH I'D BROUGHT MY SLAVEGIRL FROM HOME... NICE LITTLE ROMAN PIECE* SHE IS!
*PAX ROMANA

CENTURION, I HAVE THE ANSWER TO ALL YOUR PROBLEMS!
?!

WHO LET YOU INTO THIS CAMP, GAUL?
THE MAN ON DUTY AT THE GATE. HE WAS QUITE HAPPY WHEN I OFFERED HIM A SLAVE IN EXCHANGE!

WHO ARE YOU, ANYWAY? HOW DARE YOU CORRUPT MY LEGIONARIES?
I'M FROM MAJESTIX, RIGHTFUL CHIEF OF THE RIGHT SIDE OF OUR VILLAGE. I'M HIS ALTER EGO AND RIGHT HAND!
TAP, TAP!

AND THIS IS MY LEFT FOOT! BE OFF, OR IT'LL ALTER YOUR EGO!
CHIEF MAJESTIX WANTS YOU TO HELP HIM PUT DOWN A REBELLION LED BY CLEVERDIX!

THAT'S NONE OF MY BUSINESS! THIS IS YOUR NUNC DIMITTIS... GET OUT, OR YOU'LL BE SINGING A DIFFERENT TUNE. A FUNERAL DIRGE FROM HYMNS ANCIENT*!
*HYMNS MODERN AS YET UNWRITTEN

HOLD ON A MOMENT, CENTURION! IF YOU HELP MY CHIEF CLEVERDIX AND HIS MEN WILL BE CONQUERED... SO YOU CAN MAKE THEM YOUR **SLAVES!** YOUR LEGIONARIES ARE VERY KEEN ON HAVING SLAVES!

AND WHAT ABOUT CAESAR'S ORDERS, EH, GAUL?
NEVER MIND THAT, ROMAN! JUST THINK: HALF THE VILLAGE FIGHTING FOR YOU, THE OTHER HALF SERVING YOU AS SLAVES!

THAT'S ALL A LOAD OF COD! I'VE GOT OTHER FISH TO FRY. GET MOVING BEFORE I PUT YOU ON FATIGUES YOURSELF!
15A

RESTORE OUR DIFFERENTIALS! GIVE US SLAVES!
LEGIONARIES' LIB!
NO MORE CHORES!
SCRUB THOSE SCRUBBING BRUSHES
?!

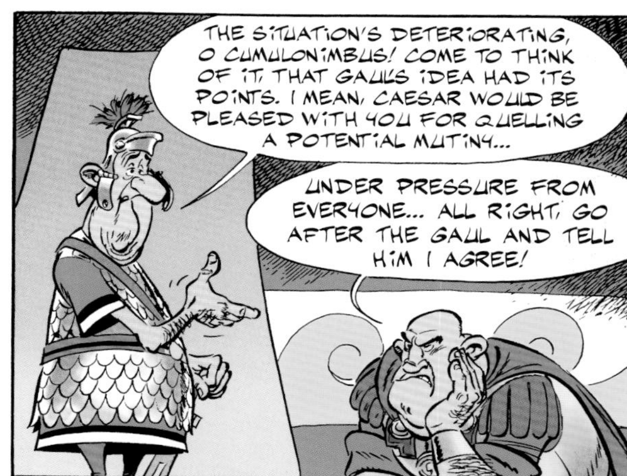
THE SITUATION'S DETERIORATING, O CUMULONIMBUS! COME TO THINK OF IT, THAT GAUL'S IDEA HAD ITS POINTS. I MEAN, CAESAR WOULD BE PLEASED WITH YOU FOR QUELLING A POTENTIAL MUTINY...
UNDER PRESSURE FROM EVERYONE... ALL RIGHT, GO AFTER THE GAUL AND TELL HIM I AGREE!

HALT!
IF YOU WANT TO LEAVE THE CAMP YOU'LL HAVE TO PROMISE ME ANOTHER SLAVE!
WAIT A MOMENT, GAUL!
15B

GO AND TELL YOUR CHIEF THAT WE'LL GIVE HIM THE HELP HE WANTS. JUST LET US HAVE TIME TO EXPLAIN IT ALL TO OUR LEGIONARIES!

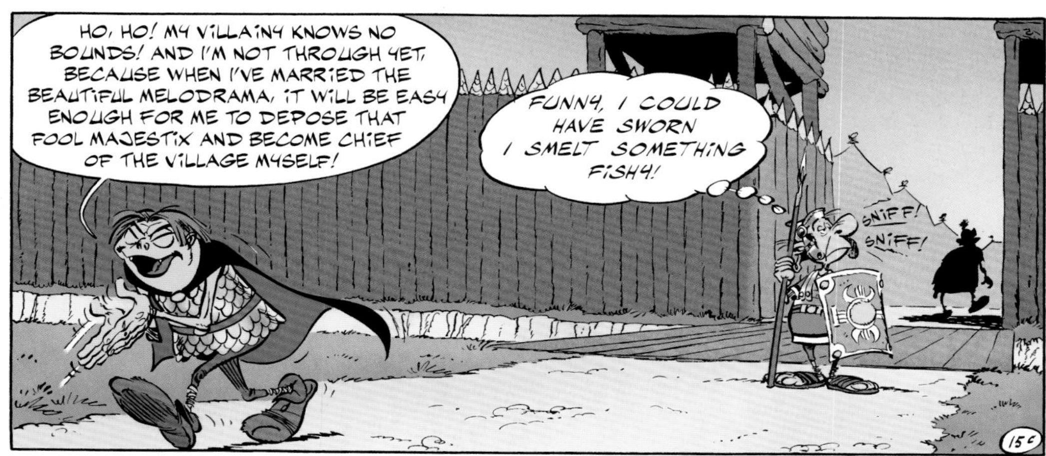
HO, HO! MY VILLAINY KNOWS NO BOUNDS! AND I'M NOT THROUGH YET, BECAUSE WHEN I'VE MARRIED THE BEAUTIFUL MELODRAMA, IT WILL BE EASY ENOUGH FOR ME TO DEPOSE THAT FOOL MAJESTIX AND BECOME CHIEF OF THE VILLAGE MYSELF!
FUNNY, I COULD HAVE SWORN I SMELT SOMETHING FISHY!
SNIFF! SNIFF!
15C

WHY, YOUR VILLAGE LOOKS MORE PEACEFUL THAN OURS!
YES, I DON'T WANT TO CRY STINKING FISH, BUT THE AIR CERTAINLY SEEMS CLEARER HERE!

DON'T YOU BELIEVE IT. THERE'S A SLUMBERING VOLCANO UNDER THOSE THATCHED ROOFS... ONE WHICH COULD ERUPT INTO VIOLENCE AT ANY MOMENT!

???
RSPRRRR!

TAP! TAP! TAP!

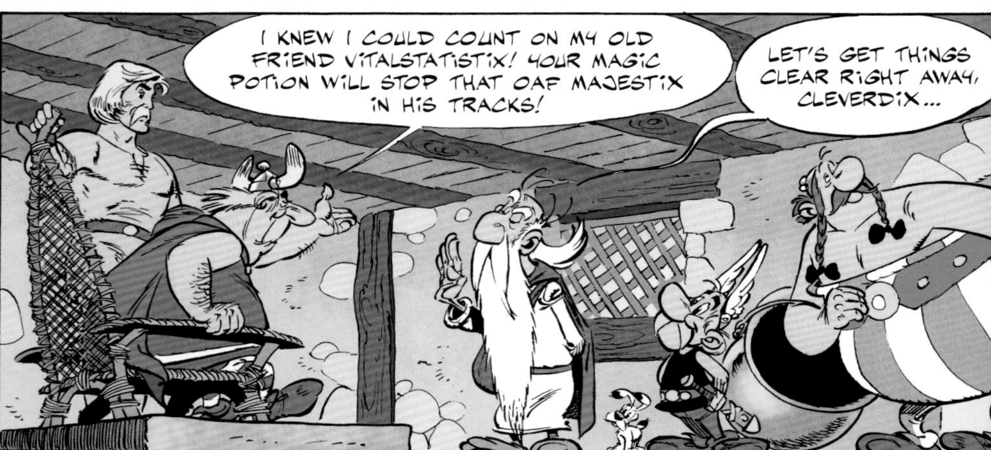
I KNEW I COULD COUNT ON MY OLD FRIEND VITALSTATISTIX! YOUR MAGIC POTION WILL STOP THAT OAF MAJESTIX IN HIS TRACKS!
LET'S GET THINGS CLEAR RIGHT AWAY, CLEVERDIX...

I DOLE OUT MAGIC POTION ONLY FOR FIGHTING ROMANS, NEVER FOR USE IN QUARRELS BETWEEN GAULS!

BUT WHAT CAN WE DO IF MAJESTIX AND HIS WARRIORS ARE FIGHTING SIDE BY SIDE WITH THE ROMANS?
THINGS HAVEN'T COME TO THAT YET, AND WHILE WE'RE WAITING FOR THE ROMANS TO COME...

THE ROMANS ARE COMING! THE ROMANS ARE COMING!!!

THE ROMANS ARE ADVANCING TOWARDS THE VILLAGE! YOU CAN GET MELODRAMA'S DOWRY READY, MAJESTIX!
RIGHT! CALL ALL OUR WARRIORS TOGETHER! WE WILL GO OUT AND WELCOME THE ROMANS!

AND TELL OUR MEN TO LEAVE THEIR WEAPONS AT HOME. WE MUST SHOW THAT WE COME IN GOOD FAITH!

HURRAH! OFF TO THE SLAVE MARKET! I'M SLAVERING WITH ANTICIPATION!
YEAH! NO MORE FATIGUES FOR US, AND I'M HANDING BACK THOSE THREE SENTRY DUTIES YOU SWAPPED ME FOR ONE COOKHOUSE FATIGUE!

SHALL WE GET THEM, ASTERIX?
WAIT A MOMENT, OBELIX! NOT YET.
SEE THAT, DRUID? WE REALLY DO NEED YOUR MAGIC POTION!
I'M AFRAID IT'S TOO LATE TO MAKE ANY NOW...
17A

WELCOME, O ROMAN! OUR GRATITUDE FOR YOUR VALUABLE ASSISTANCE KNOWS NO BOUNDS, AND...
CUT THE CACKLE! WHERE ARE THE SLAVES?

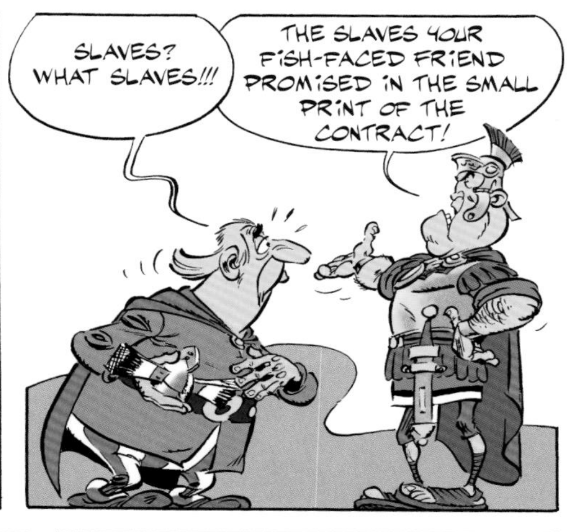
SLAVES? WHAT SLAVES!!!
THE SLAVES YOUR FISH-FACED FRIEND PROMISED IN THE SMALL PRINT OF THE CONTRACT!

GAULS NEVER, NEVER, NEVER WILL BE SLAVES! I SHALL BE CHIEF OF EVERYONE IN THE VILLAGE WITHOUT EXCEPTION, AND WITHOUT SLAVES!
YOU DON'T GO CALLING OUT THE ROMAN ARMY FOR NOTHING! MEN, GRAB HOLD OF THIS LOT! THEY CAN BE OUR SLAVES THEMSELVES!

HELP! THAT FOOL MAJESTIX HAS RUINED EVERYTHING!
17B

YOU KNOW, FATHER, MAJESTIX REALLY DID ACT IN A MANNER WORTHY OF A CHIEF!
ALL THINGS CONSIDERED, I MUST ADMIT HE CARRIED IT OFF IN STYLE!

WE'LL GET THEM THIS TIME, ASTERIX!!!
NO, OBELIX! IT COULD PUT MAJESTIX AND HIS WARRIORS IN DANGER!

A LITTLE LATER...
WE MUST DO SOMETHING, HISTRIONIX!
SNIFF!
HUH!
DON'T WORRY, MELODRAMA! IF MY FATHER WILL AGREE, WE'LL ORGANIZE A CAMPAIGN AGAINST THE ROMANS TO FREE OUR FELLOW VILLAGERS!
I CERTAINLY AGREE! MAJESTIX MAY BE MY OPPONENT, BUT I DON'T WANT HIM USING HIS SACRIFICE AS AN ARGUMENT AT THE POLLS!

WAIT A MOMENT! I'VE GOT A BETTER IDEA!

THE ROMANS OF THESE PARTS DON'T KNOW GETAFIX, OBELIX AND ME. WE'LL GO TO THE ROMAN CAMP ON OUR OWN, IF IT'S SLAVES THEY WANT, WE'LL APPLY FOR THE JOB, AND SET THE PRISONERS FREE!
AN EXCELLENT IDEA, ASTERIX!
OOH, YES! GOODY, GOODY, GOODY! A CHANCE TO SAMPLE THE LOCAL ROMANS AT LAST...
CLAP! CLAP! CLAP!

... THUMPING ROMANS IS LIKE HAVING DINNER: IT'S NICE TO EAT OUT FOR A CHANGE!

…N THE ROMAN
…AMP...
WE WILL NEVER BE YOUR SLAVES, ROMAN!
DO YOU KNOW THE PENALTIES FOR A SLAVES' REVOLT? YOU'D BETTER STOP AND THINK, UNLESS YOU WANT TO MAKE THE LIONS IN THE CIRCUS MAXIMUS AT ROME A SQUARE MEAL!

AND WHILE THEY'RE THINKING, CHAIN THEM ALL UP WELL!!!

CAN I HAVE THOSE THREE SENTRY DUTIES BACK? THE ONES YOU SWAPPED FOR MY COOKHOUSE FATIGUE!
PRICES HAVE RISEN... IT'LL BE FOUR SENTRY DUTIES NOW!

MEANWHILE...
GOOD LUCK, FRIENDS!
DON'T WORRY, MELODRAMA! THANKS TO GETAFIX'S KNOW-HOW, OBELIX'S STRENGTH, DOGMATIX'S NOSE AND MY CUNNING, WE'LL SOON HAVE YOUR FATHER HOME!

FUNNY HOW SURE OF THEMSELVES CLEVERDIX'S ALLIES SEEM! I'LL FOLLOW THEM AT A SAFE DISTANCE!

DOGMATIX HAS BEEN SNIFFING ABOUT EVER SINCE WE LEFT! I THINK HE'S PICKED UP THE SCENT OF A BOAR!
NO, NO, IT'S JUST A RED HERRING.
SNIFF SNIFF SNIFF

IF SO, IT'S BEEN TAKING CODLIVER OIL!
SNIFF! SNIFF!

RIGHT, YOU GET THE IDEA, OBELIX? WE'RE HUMBLE SLAVES, SO NO THUMPING THE ROMANS!
LISTEN, ASTERIX...

...IS THERE SUCH A THING AS A SLAVE-DOG?

HALT!
WHO GOES THERE, AND WHAT DO YOU WANT?
GAULISH SLAVES, AND WE WANT TO SERVE THE ROMAN ARMY!

THAT'S A BIT OF LUCK! WE'VE JUST GOT SOME BRAND-NEW SLAVES IN, BUT THEY WON'T SERVE YET!

AND I'LL KEEP THIS FAT SLAVE FOR MYSELF!

BONK!

I MAY BE A SLAVE, BUT
I AM NOT FAT!
TAP! TAP! TAP!
TAP! TAP! TAP!

WELL, JUST HOW DO YOU EXPECT THEM TO TAKE US SERIOUSLY NOW, OBELIX?
I THINK I CAN FIX IT...

THIS FLASK CONTAINS AN ELIXIR OF MY OWN INVENTION! A FEW DROPS WILL INSTANTLY RESTORE THIS ROMAN TO FULL HEALTH AND STRENGTH...

AND HE WON'T EVEN REMEMBER WHAT HAPPENED!

HALT!
WHO GOES THERE, AND WHAT DO YOU WANT?
GAULISH SLAVES, AND WE WANT TO SERVE THE ROMAN ARMY!
HERE WE GO AGAIN...
AMAZING! THOSE GAULS ARE AMAZING... AND I CAN'T HELP WONDERING WHAT TRICK THEY'RE PLAN-NING TO PLAY ON THE ROMANS!

AND I'LL KEEP THIS FA...
NO! DON'T!

SO SORRY, WE'RE CLASS I SLAVES, AND WE CAN'T SERVE THE RANK AND FILE!
?!?

HOW DID HE GUESS WHAT I WAS GOING TO SAY?

THE DRUID FORGOT HIS FLASK! I ABSOLUTELY MUST GET HOLD OF IT. IT COULD COME IN USEFUL!
21A

ALWAYS THE SAME OLD STORY! THE RANK AND FILE DON'T HAVE ANY RIGHT TO...

CLANG!

NOW TO OBSERVE DEVELOPMENTS DISCREETLY! I FIND THESE GAULS MORE AND MORE INTRIGUING!

THREE NEW GAULS HAVE JUST ARRIVED, CUMULONIMBUS! THEY WANT TO BE YOUR SLAVES.
?!? I SHALL CERTAINLY NEVER UNDERSTAND THE GAULS!

O ROMAN, I AND MY FRIENDS HAVE COME TO OFFER YOU OUR CULINARY SKILLS! NAME YOUR DISH, AND I CAN COOK IT TO PERFECTION. JUST ORDER THE MENU, AND SEE WHAT HAPPENS!
21B

THE GODS MUST HAVE SENT YOU, GAUL! A SPOT OF GOOD COOKING WILL CERTAINLY MAKE A CHANGE FROM THE USUAL MESS!
OH, WE CAN COOK A GOOD MEAL FOR ALL YOUR MEN, CENTURION! THE FEAST OF THE CENTURY, AS YOU MIGHT SAY!

FOR STARTERS, A FORTIFYING SOUP. THE MEAT COURSE... A REALLY NICE CUT! SAY CHUMP CHOP, STEWED IN YOUR... I MEAN, IN ITS OWN JUICE. AND WE WON'T MAKE A HASH OF IT. IF YOU FANCY POULTRY, WE CAN COOK YOUR GOOSE FOR YOU! GAME FOR ANYTHING? THEN GROUSE AND QUAIL. AFTER THAT, YOU GET YOUR DESSERTS: A FOOL, WELL BEATEN, PERHAPS SOME INSTANT WHIP, AND A FEW RASPBERRIES. ALL WASHED DOWN WITH THE GAULISH BEER WE CALL WALLOP... IT PACKS QUITE A PUNCH!

THAT'LL DO FINE! GET ON WITH IT... I CAN HARDLY WAIT!
WE SHAN'T TAKE LONG!
WINK

LOOK HERE, GETAFIX, WHY DON'T WE ADD A FEW NICE ROAST BOARS?
?!? WHY NOT GO AND CHOP UP SOME KINDLING FOR THE FIRE, OBELIX?

WELL, I ONLY THOUGHT HE'D GONE AND FORGOTTEN THE BOARS...

!
CHOP, CHOP, CHOP, CHOP,

AMAZING! I'VE NEVER SEEN ANYONE CHOP WOOD LIKE THAT BEFORE!
OH, THAT'S NOTHING! I COULD CUT A WHOLE TREE DOWN THAT WAY, ONLY DOGMATIX WOULDN'T LIKE IT!

SOON AFTERWARDS...
READY IN A MOMENT!
I'M A BIT WORRIED, CENTURION! A COUSIN OF MINE STATIONED IN ARMORICA TOLD ME ABOUT A DRUID THERE WHO HAS STRANGE POWERS, AND I'M JUST WONDERING WHETHER...
YOU'VE GOT A POINT, INFECTIUS VIRUS. WE MUST BE CAREFUL!

WOULD YOU LIKE TO TASTE THE SOUP FOR SEASONING, CENTURION?
JUST A MOMENT, GAUL! HOW DO I KNOW YOU'RE NOT TRYING TO POISON THE GARRISON, SO AS TO SET THE PRISONERS FREE?

I QUITE UNDERSTAND YOUR FEELINGS. YOU DON'T WANT TO FIND YOURSELF IN THE SOUP. SO WE'LL DRINK SOME OURSELVES, TO SHOW IT'S ALL RIGHT!
AND TO PROVE IT EVEN MORE CONCLUSIVELY, WE'LL GIVE SOME TO THE PRISONERS TOO!

GLUGGLUGGLUG

GLUGGLUGGLUG

NO, OBELIX, NOT YOU!

AND WHY NOT HIM?
YES, WHY NOT ME?
BECAUSE HE FELL INTO THE CAULDRON WHEN HE WAS A BABY, AND... ER... UM...

AND HE HAS TO STAY ON A STRICT DIET FOR THE GOOD OF HIS MENTAL HEALTH, THAT'S WHY NOT HIM!
23A

DON'T WORRY, WE'RE HERE TO RESCUE YOU. THE POTION WILL GIVE YOU THE STRENGTH YOU NEED. WATCH FOR OUR SIGNAL! THEN YOU HAVE NOTHING TO LOSE BUT YOUR CHAINS!
?!

SOON AFTERWARDS...
YOU SEE, ROMAN, THERE WAS NO NEED FOR YOU TO WORRY!
WELL, SINCE THERE ISN'T ANY SOUP LEFT, LET'S GO STRAIGHT ON TO THE NEXT COURSE ON THE MENU, WHICH IS...

THE CHOP!
PAF!

THE MENU! I SEE IT ALL NOW!!!

SO DO WE! COME ON, MEN!
SNAP!
23B

THAT POTION OF YOURS HAS A REALLY UPLIFTING EFFECT!
YES, IT USUALLY MAKES PEOPLE RISE TO THE OCCASION!
TRY A BIT OF KNUCKLE IN THE BREAD-BASKET FOR A CHANGE!
ENJOYING YOUR PICNIC AL FRESCO?
GRRR!

I GET THE PICTURE... NO NEED FOR ANY BIG FRESCO TO SHOW THAT THE ROMANS CAN'T STOMACH THAT DRUID'S RECIPES!

GAULISH COOKING! HUH! THEY CAN SCOFF THE LOT THEMSELVES!
PERSONALLY, I DON'T SEE ANYTHING TO SCOFF AT.
SSH! SHUT UP! THEY MIGHT WANT TO CARVE US UP SOME MORE.
I DON'T KNOW WHO YOU ARE, BUT THANKS VERY MUCH! YOU CAME IN THE NICK OF TIME!
I'M GETAFIX, AND MY FRIENDS HERE ARE ASTERIX, OBELIX AND DOGMATIX. CLEVERDIX SENT US!

CLEVERDIX WANTED TO FIGHT THE ROMANS WITH HIS OWN WARRIORS, BUT WE THOUGHT OUR METHODS WERE SUBTLER!
THERE'S SOMETHING TO BE SAID FOR THAT OLD ROGUE CLEVERDIX AFTER ALL!

NOW, LET'S GO BACK TO THE VILLAGE. AND I SHALL HAVE SOMETHING TO SAY TO THAT TRAITOR CODFIX!

OH, HELP! I'D BETTER LIE LOW FOR A WHILE!

?!?

HALT!
SLAVES ARE NOT ALLOWED TO LEAVE THE CAMP!

THAT'S ALL RIGHT, WE'RE NOT SLAVES ANY MORE. WE'RE FREE GAULS AGAIN! YOU CAN LET US PASS!
HUH! AS LIARS GO, YOU'RE A FAT LOT OF GOOD!

LEAVE THIS TO ME, ASTERIX!

GOOD I MAY BE, BUT I... AM... NOT... FAT!
TCHAC!
25A

JUST NICELY COVERED, THAT'S ALL.
WELL, YOU'RE CERTAINLY VERY THIN-SKINNED! COME ON, OBELIX!

O DRUID, WASN'T IT A BIT DANGEROUS TO GIVE THE ROMANS A CHANCE TO DRINK OUR MAGIC POTION TOO?
THAT WAS A RISK WE HAD TO TAKE. I HAD EVERY CONFIDENCE IN THE ROMANS' LACK OF CONFIDENCE IN US, ASTERIX!

OH, FATHER!
MELODRAMA, MY DEAR CHILD!
25B

IT WAS ALL BECAUSE OF THAT DREADFUL CODFIX!
YES, AND WHERE'S THE TWO-TIMING SO-AND-SO NOW?

HE DISAPPEARED WHEN YOU LEFT.
HUH! HE'LL BE LOOKING PRETTY GREEN AROUND THE GILLS WHEN I FIND HIM!

YOU KNOW, I FEEL CODFIX MAY STILL BE FISHING IN THESE TROUBLED WATERS!
YES. WE DON'T WANT HIM TURNING THE SCALES...

OUR OWN QUARREL ISN'T SETTLED YET, YOU KNOW, YOU ROTTEN OLD FRAUD!
IT CERTAINLY ISN'T! AND THIS TIME IT'LL BE A FAIR FIGHT, YOU ROTTEN OLD OPPORTUNIST!

YES, WELL, MEANWHILE YOU'D BETTER BARRICADE YOURSELVES INSIDE THE VILLAGE, IN CASE THE ROMANS DECIDE TO COME BACK!
AND I'M GOING TO BREW UP SOME MAGIC POTION... ONLY TO BE TAKEN IF THE ROMANS DO COME BACK, OF COURSE!

JUST AT THAT MOMENT, HOWEVER, THE ROMANS HAVE NOT RECOVERED FROM THEIR LITTLE SETBACK. MEANWHILE...
NOW THAT THE WHOLE VILLAGE IS AGAINST ME, I'D BETTER MAKE USE OF THE ROMANS TO SATISFY MY THIRST FOR VENGEANCE...

...AND A FEW DROPS OF THE DRUID'S ELIXIR, ADDED TO THIS WINE, WILL HELP ME WHEN THE CENTURION COMES TO SATISFY HIS THIRST!

SOUND THE ASSEMBLY!

RiGHT! WE SHALL NOW FORGET THiS WHOLE UNFORTUNATE EPiSODE AND CLEAR UP THE MESS! I WANT THE GARRiSON ALL SPRUCED UP AND LOOKiNG LiKE A CENA CANiS*! DiSMiSS!
* LATIN: DOG'S DINNER

WHAT'S CENA CANiS?
DOG LATIN, YOU iDIOT!

AH, A NiCE GOBLET OF WiNE WiLL HELP ME FORGET MY TROUBLES!

GLUG! GLUG! GLUG!

AAAAAH! BY JUPiTER, I'M FEELiNG ON TOP OF THE WORLD!
27A

?!? WHO ARE YOU, GAUL, AND WHO LET YOU iNTO THiS CAMP?
IT'S WORKiNG!

I'VE COME TO WARN YOU, O CENTURiON! THE GAULS OF THE NEARBY ViLLAGE HAVE BROKEN THE PAX ROMANA! THEY'VE BASHED UP YOUR LEGIONARiES AND RANSACKED YOUR CAMP!
IMPOSSiBLE! OR ARE YOU GiViNG ME SOME iNSiDE DOPE?

O CUMULONiMBUS, THE MEN DON'T WANT TO CLEAR UP THE MESS! THEY'RE ALL REPORTiNG SiCK!

SiCK BAY
27B

SOUND THE ASSEMBLY! I WANT THIS GARRISON PLACED ON A WAR FOOTING!

TANTANTARAA!
THOSE GAULS WILL FIND OUT WHAT BREAKING THE PAX ROMANA MEANS!

TARAA...
BOING!
?!?

REQUIESCAMUS IN PACE!
PILUM POWER? NO THANKS!
FIGHT WAR NOT GAULS!

I KNOW HOW TO STRAIGHTEN ALL THIS OUT. SEND FOR AN AMPHORA OF WINE! YOU WON'T REGRET IT!

?!?

EXTRA GROG RATION COMING UP!

TAKE IT EASY. THERE'LL BE PLENTY FOR EVERYONE!

BY JUPITER, I'M FEELING GREAT! NOT AT ALL GROGGY!
THIS IS A RUM DO... WHO MIGHT YOU BE?

AND LATER...
I STILL HAVE NO IDEA WHO YOU ARE, GAUL, BUT YOU WON'T FIND ME UNGRATEFUL FOR SERVICES RENDERED!
WE CAN TALK ABOUT THAT LATER, ONCE YOU'VE DONE FOR THE VILLAGE AND ALL ITS INHABITANTS.

BUT WATCH OUT! THERE'S A DRUID WITH THEM, AND HE HAS A POTION WHICH MAKES ANYONE WHO DRINKS IT INVINCIBLE!

CENTURION, A COUSIN OF MINE STATIONED IN ARMORICA TOLD ME ABOUT A DRUID THERE WHO HAS STRANGE POWERS, AND I'M JUST WONDERING WHETHER...
YOU'VE GOT A POINT, INFECTIUS VIRUS! WE MUST BE CAREFUL!

MEANWHILE, IN THE GAULISH VILLAGE...
THE MAGIC POTION'S READY. WE'D BETTER PUT IT SAFE ON NEUTRAL GROUND SOMEWHERE WHILE WE WAIT TO SEE IF THE ROMANS ARE COMING BACK!
SCHIZOPHRENIX'S HUT IS NEUTRAL GROUND. IT'S BANG IN THE MIDDLE OF THE VILLAGE.
29A

YES, LET'S PUT IT THERE. THAT FOOL SCHIZOPHRENIX HAS NEVER BEEN ABLE TO DECIDE WHICH SIDE HE'S ON!

DIDN'T YOU EVER THINK OF PUTTING FLOOR-BOARDS DOWN OVER THE GAP?
THAT'S FLOORED HIM! WE'LL DO IT NOW.

ND SO, A ITTLE LATER...
I'LL WATCH OVER THE CAULDRON TONIGHT, TO MAKE DOUBLY SURE!

THEN YOU'D BETTER HAVE THIS GOURD OF MAGIC POTION, ASTERIX. YOU NEVER KNOW, YOU MIGHT NEED A BOOSTER DOSE, IN SPITE OF THE POTION IN THE CAULDRON.
29B

AND THAT NIGHT, ON THE OUTSKIRTS OF THE WOOD NEAR THE GAULISH VILLAGE...
I DON'T TRUST THAT DRUID AND HIS SECRET WEAPONS! I THINK I'D BETTER GO SCOUTING AHEAD BEFORE WE ATTACK!

AND WHATEVER YOU DO, DON'T MOVE TILL I GET BACK!
RIGHT, BUT HURRY UP! I CAN'T WAIT TO GET MY REVENGE ON THOSE GAULS!

THE GODS OF THE UNDERWORLD ARE ON MY SIDE! IT'S THAT FOOL CONGENITALIDIOTIX ON SENTRY DUTY! I'LL SOON DEAL WITH HIM!

HALT! WHO GOES THERE?
IT'S ME. CODFIX.

I MIGHT HAVE KNOWN FROM THE SMELL! WHAT DO YOU WANT?
I WANT TO ASK CHIEF MAJESTIX TO FORGIVE ME!

YOU CAN COME IN, BUT IF I WERE YOU I'D KEEP MY DISTANCE FROM MAJESTIX!
WHY ARE YOU MOUNTING GUARD LIKE THIS? WHAT ARE YOU AFRAID OF?

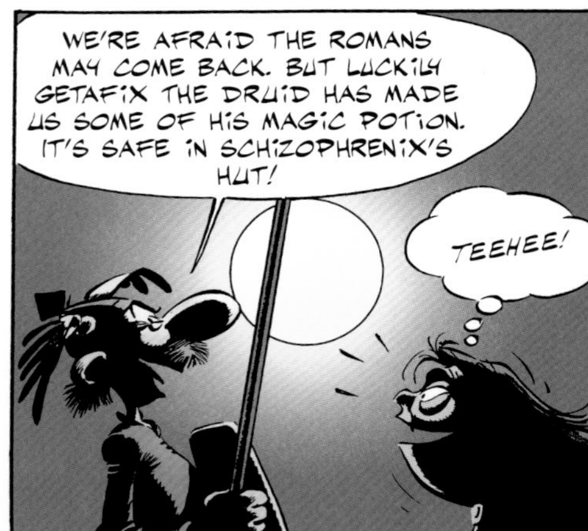
WE'RE AFRAID THE ROMANS MAY COME BACK. BUT LUCKILY GETAFIX THE DRUID HAS MADE US SOME OF HIS MAGIC POTION. IT'S SAFE IN SCHIZOPHRENIX'S HUT!
TEEHEE!

I'VE NEVER BEEN ABLE TO SEE STARS INSIDE A HUT BEFORE!

BONG!

I'M SURE I SHALL NEED SOME OF THIS!

I FEEL QUITE SORRY FOR CODFIX, APOLOGIZING TO THE CHIEF.. HE MUST BE HAVING TO STEEL HIMSELF WONDER IF HE'LL GET AWAY WITH IT?

?!
CRAAASH!

HELP! HELP!
31A

DO SOMETHING, GETAFIX! GIVE HIM SOME OF THE ELIXIR YOU USED ON THE ROMANS!
I'M SORRY, MY DEAR OBELIX, I'M AFRAID I MUST HAVE LEFT IT NEAR THE ROMAN CAMP!

ANYWAY, IT WOULD BE DANGEROUS TO GIVE IT TO ASTERIX. ANYONE WHO DRINKS MY ELIXIR CAN'T TAKE THE MAGIC POTION AFTERWARDS... THE MIXTURE HAS SOME RATHER STRANGE EFFECTS!

BUT LUCKILY ASTERIX IS ALL RIGHT!
THIS TIME I REALLY DO THINK THE SKY HAS FALLEN ON MY HEAD!

THE SKY'S FALLEN ON EVERYONE'S HEAD, ASTERIX! CODFIX HAS STOLEN THE MAGIC POTION, AND HE'S SURE TO DOSE THE ROMANS WITH IT.

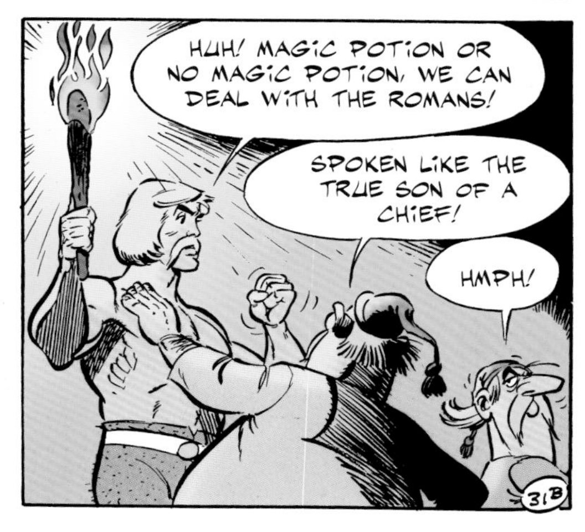
HUH! MAGIC POTION OR NO MAGIC POTION, WE CAN DEAL WITH THE ROMANS!
SPOKEN LIKE THE TRUE SON OF A CHIEF!
HMPH!
31B

THE SUN'S COMING UP! YOU TOOK YOUR TIME, GAUL! I THOUGHT YOU WERE PLANNING TO BETRAY US!
BETRAY YOU? LOOK WHAT I'VE GOT HERE! THE MAGIC POTION WHICH MAKES ANYONE WHO DRINKS IT INVINCIBLE!

ARE YOU SURE IT'S...
WATCH THIS!

CRAAACK!
!
!
!
!
!
!
!

CLAPCLAPCLAPCLAPCLAPCLAPCLAPCLAPCLAPCLA

NEVER MIND THE CURTAIN CALLS! IT'LL BE CURTAINS FOR US IF WE DON'T GET ON WITH DRINKING IT!

SOON AFTERWARDS...
THAT'S IT! EVERYONE'S HAD HIS POTION. COMING TO JOIN THE ATTACK?
ER... NO... NO, IT WOULD BE BETTER FOR ME NOT TO BE SEEN WITH YOU! IT'S A MATTER OF PRINCIPLE, YOU KNOW!

FORWARD MARCH!

I MAY STILL JUST HAVE TIME TO BREW UP SOME MORE PO...
THE ROMANS ARE COMING!

WE MUST GO OUT TO MEET THE ROMANS AND FIGHT THEM, IF WE'RE TO SAVE THE VILLAGE!

I THINK WE'RE IN FOR SOME MORE FUN, ASTERIX!

WELL, THE ROMANS HAVE DRUNK THE MAGIC POTION, OBELIX. THAT MEANS WE MUST HANDLE THEM MORE CAREFULLY!
DON'T WORRY, ASTERIX. I'LL HANDLE THE ROMANS EVER SO CAREFULLY!

COME ON, MEN! FOR ROME, HOME AND BEAUTY!
I SEEM TO BE SWELLING WITH PRIDE...

WHAT... WHAT... WHAT THE... ???
?
?
?
?
?
33A

THAT GAUL BETRAYED US! HE WAS MAKING FUN OF US!
YES, HE WAS SENDING US UP...

GETAFIX, LOOK AT THOSE ROMANS! THEY'VE GONE ALL ROUND AND AIRBORNE!
TEEHEE! I'M NOT A BIT SURPRISED. THAT'S THE EFFECT OF TAKING MAGIC POTION ON TOP OF THE ELIXIR! OBELIX IS RIGHT; THE ROMANS ARE GOING TO GIVE US SOME FUN!

WELL, IF THIS IS A JOKE, IT'S BLOWN UP OUT OF ALL PRO-PORTION!
I DON'T LIKE SUCH LEVITY!
HELP! THIS IS A WHOLE NEW BALL GAME!
BONG!
BONG!
BONG!
BONG!
BONG!
BONG!
BONG!

COME ON, CHARGE!
33B

BLAM

BONG!

THESE ROMANS ARE REALLY CRAZY! THEY'RE NOT AT THE CIRCUS NOW!

AND MEANWHILE...

BING!

BANG!

BONG!

AHA! NO MORE GLOBE-TROTTING! WE'RE BACK TO NORMAL!

PICK UP YOUR WEAPONS AND GET BACK TO BATTLE STATIONS!!!
35A

O CUMULONIMBUS, I'M AN OLD SOLDIER, AND I'VE BEEN AROUND, BUT I'VE NEVER FOUGHT IN TERRAIN QUITE LIKE THIS!
I'LL TELL YOU ANOTHER FUNNY THING... WE'VE LOST SIGHT OF THE ENEMY!
BUT WE'RE STILL HERE, O ROMAN!
?!?
EEEEK!

35B

GIANTS! THEY'RE GIANTS!

NO, WE AREN'T! YOU'RE THE ONES WHO'VE SHRUNK! IN FUTURE YOU'LL KNOW BETTER THAN TO TAKE MAGIC POTION WITHOUT A DRUID'S PRESCRIPTION!

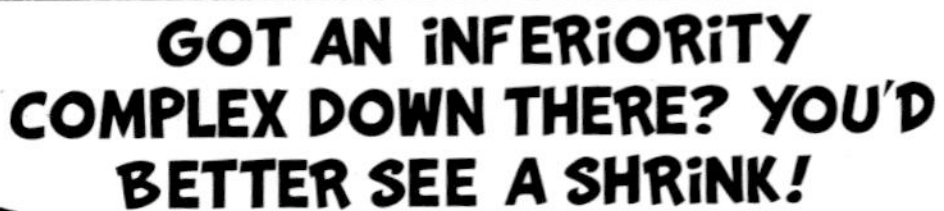

GOT AN INFERIORITY COMPLEX DOWN THERE? YOU'D BETTER SEE A SHRINK!

MERCY! BY ALL THE GODS, MAKE THIS NIGHTMARE STOP!

YOU'LL SOON BE BACK TO YOUR NORM SIZE, BUT FIRST YO MUST SWEAR TO LEA THE VILLAGE AND IT PEOPLE IN PEACE!
I SWEAR! MAY I FADE AWAY IF I BREAK MY OATH!

OFF YOU GO BACK TO CAMP, ROMANS, AND MIND WE NEVER FIND YOU IN THIS NEIGHBOURHOOD AGAIN!

NOW HURRY UP AND GET OUT, BEFORE DOGMATIX DECIDES YOU'D MAKE A TASTY MORSEL OR SO!
GRRRRRRRRR

HA HA!
HA HA HA!
HA HA HA HA!
WOOF! WOOF!

WELL, MY DEAR OBELIX, YOU STARTED QUITE A TRAIN OF EVENTS WITH THAT PUNCH YOU GAVE THE SENTRY OUTSIDE THE ROMAN CAMP.. AND THE ENEMY LOST OUT!
YOU MEAN I DID IT?

ER... MAJESTIX, NOW WE'VE DEALT WITH THE ROMANS, I... THERE'S SOMETHING I'D LIKE TO ASK YOU...
JUST A MOMENT, MY BOY! DON'T FORGET YOUR FATHER AND I STILL HAVE TO SETTLE OUR ARGUMENT, AND...

MAJESTIX! MAJESTIX!
?!

CODFIX HAS KIDNAPPED MELODRAMA! HE LEFT THIS ROLL OF PARCHMENT ADDRESSED TO YOU!
THE DOUBLE-DEALING TRAITOR!
37A

IF YOU WANT TO SEE MELODRAMA AGAIN, LEAVE 100 POUNDS IN GOLD NEAR THE DOLMEN BY THE SPRING BEFORE SUNSET. CODFIX

THE VILLAIN! I'M REALLY IN A JAM NOW, AND SO IS MELODRAMA... IT'S ALL VERY WELL FOR CODFIX*, BUT WHERE DO I GET THAT KIND OF MONEY BY SUNSET?
I SHALL LEAVE AT ONCE IN SEARCH OF CODFIX, AND BY TOUTATIS, I SWEAR TO BRING MELODRAMA BACK SAFE AND SOUND!
*HENCE: MONEY FOR JAM.

OBELIX AND I WILL GO WITH YOU...

SO WILL DOGMATIX! LOOK, HE'S ALREADY PICKED UP THE SCENT! HE'S MAKING STRAIGHT FOR THE RIVER!
SNIFF! SNIFF!

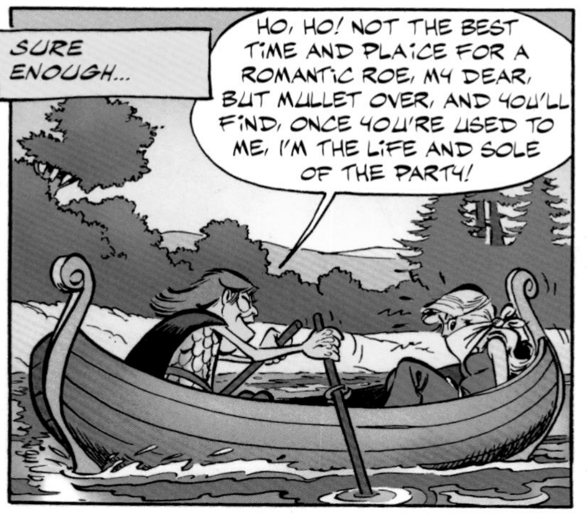
SURE ENOUGH...
HO, HO! NOT THE BEST TIME AND PLAICE FOR A ROMANTIC ROE, MY DEAR, BUT MULLET OVER, AND YOU'LL FIND, ONCE YOU'RE USED TO ME, I'M THE LIFE AND SOLE OF THE PARTY!

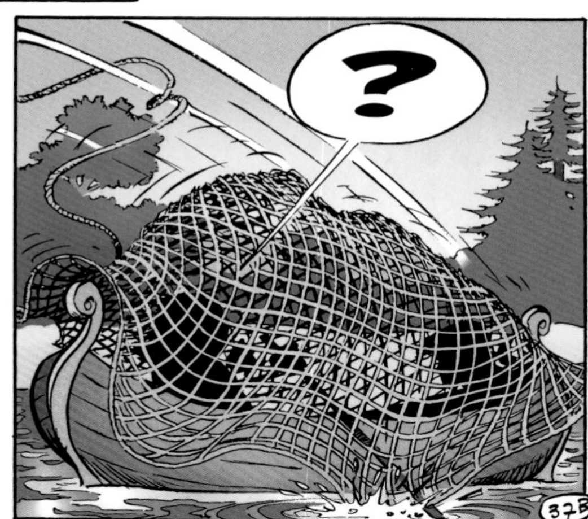
?
37B

WELL, ME HEARTIES, THERE'LL BE MANY A GOOD CATCH TO BE HAD IN THIS RIVER... HERE'S THE FIRST! AND WE CAN BE SURE WE DON'T RUN ANY RISK OF MEETING THOSE GAULS INLAND!
IF YOU BUY THAT YOU'LL BUY ANYTHING. CAVEAT EMPTOR!

I HAVE A STRAIGHTFORWARD DEAL TO SUGGEST, O PIRATE!

I'VE KIDNAPPED CHIEF MAJESTIX'S DAUGHTER, AND I'M ASKING A RANSOM OF 50 POUNDS FOR HER. WHY DON'T YOU GUARD HER WHILE I COLLECT THE RANSOM, AND THEN WE SHARE THE MONEY? ALL RIGHT?
HO, HO! YES, WHY NOT?

IT SOUNDS FISHY... SURELY YOU'RE NOT GOING SHARES WITH THAT SLIPPERY CUSTOMER?
YOU BET I'M NOT! AS SOON AS HE'S BACK WITH THE RANSOM, WE'LL DEMAND A SECOND RANSOM FOR THE GIRL AND HER KIDNAPPER! HA, HA, HA, TEE HEEHEE!

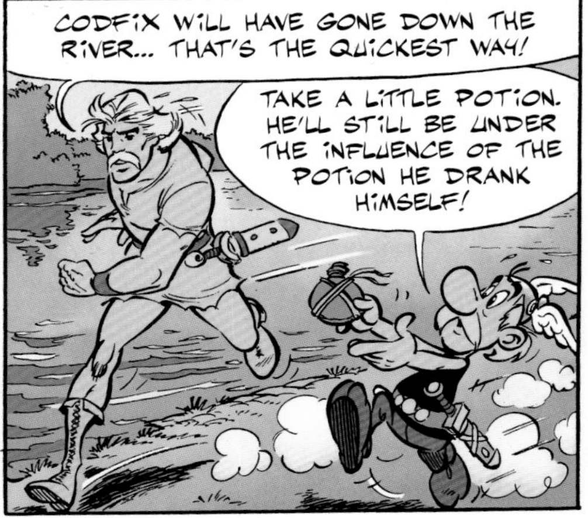
CODFIX WILL HAVE GONE DOWN THE RIVER... THAT'S THE QUICKEST WAY!
TAKE A LITTLE POTION. HE'LL STILL BE UNDER THE INFLUENCE OF THE POTION HE DRANK HIMSELF!

LOOK! A BOAT!
WHY, IF IT ISN'T OUR OLD FRIENDS! AND SOMETHING TELLS ME WE'LL FIND MELODRAMA WITH THEM!

CAP'N, YOU SAID THERE'D BE A CATCH IN IT, AND THERE IS...

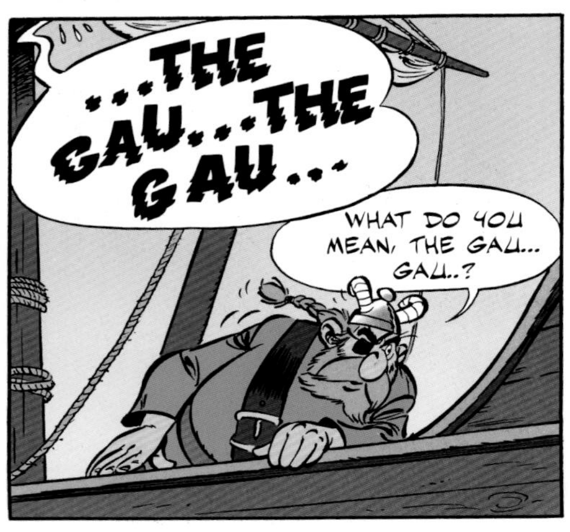
...THE GAU...THE GAU...
WHAT DO YOU MEAN, THE GAU... GAU..?

THE GAU... THE GAULS!

YOU HAVE NOTHING TO FEAR NOW, MELODRAMA!

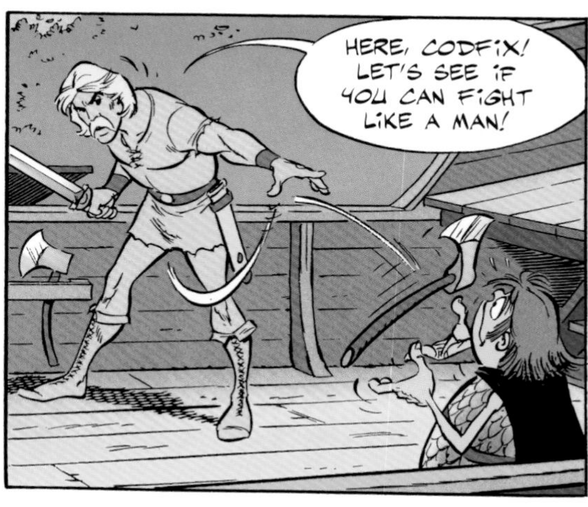
HERE, CODFIX! LET'S SEE IF YOU CAN FIGHT LIKE A MAN!

CRAACK!

WHOOSH!

THEY'RE... THEY'RE BREAKING UP MY SHIP! THEY'RE SINKING HER!
YES, HE'S GOT CODFIX HOOK, LINE AND SINKER!

D A LITTLE
TER...
THE EFFECTS OF THE MAGIC POTION HAVE WORN OFF... YOU WOULDN'T HIT A DEFENCELESS MAN WOULD YOU?

PAF!

HULLO, A FLYING FISH!

PHEW! RIGHT... THE NIGHTMARE'S OVER, AND I NEVER WANT TO HEAR A WORD ABOUT GAULS OR SLAVES AGAIN!!!

CRAASH!
PAF!
?

BY ALL THE GODS OF OLYMPUS, I'LL TAKE BACK THAT LAST REMARK OF MINE, JUST FOR YOU! I'LL GIVE YOU A JOB YOU WON'T BE LEAVING IN A HURRY!

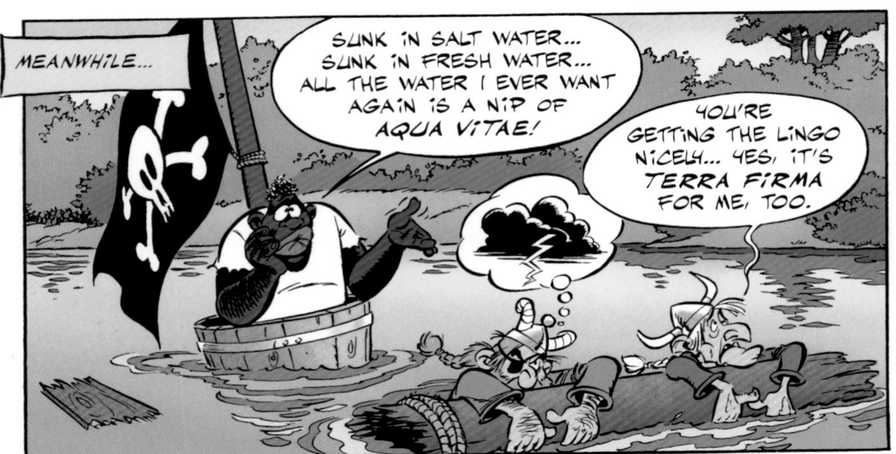
MEANWHILE...
SUNK IN SALT WATER... SUNK IN FRESH WATER... ALL THE WATER I EVER WANT AGAIN IS A NIP OF AQUA VITAE!
YOU'RE GETTING THE LINGO NICELY... YES, IT'S TERRA FIRMA FOR ME, TOO.

QUICK, LET'S GO AND SET MAJESTIX'S MIND AT REST!

IN TIMES OF TROUBLE SUCH AS THIS, IT IS ONLY RIGHT TO FORGET OUR DIFFERENCES, AND I FEEL FOR YOU, MAJESTIX!

THEY'RE BACK, WITH MELODRAMA!

OH FATHER, HISTRIONIX ACTED LIKE A TRUE CHIEF!
I'M EXTREMELY GRATEFUL TO HISTRIONIX FOR HIS BRAVE ACTION, BUT THAT'S GOING A BIT TOO FAR MY DEAR!

OH NO, IT ISN'T. AFTER ALL, HISTRIONIX IS THE SON OF A CHIEF!
SON OF A CHIEF MY FOOT!!! I'M THE ONLY REAL CHIEF AROUND HERE!

OH, FOR GOODNESS' SAKE, WE'VE HAD ENOUGH OF THIS! IF YOU MUST FIGHT FOR THE CHIEFTAINSHIP KEEP IT BETWEEN THE TWO OF YOU!!!
?!
?!

MELODRAMA IS QUITE RIGHT! FIGHT IF YOU MUST, BUT LEAVE THE OTHER VILLAGERS OUT OF IT. THEY'VE HAD ENOUGH OF YOUR QUARRELS!

AND SOON AFTERWARDS...
NOW, YOU SENILE OLD DOTARD, I'LL SHOW YOU WHAT A REAL CHIEF CAN DO, AND WITH MY BARE HANDS!
YOU DYSPEPTIC OLD FOGY! YOU'RE IN FOR A SHOCK!

YOU'LL NEED A NEUTRAL UMPIRE. I VOLUNTEER TO REFEREE YOUR SINGLE COMBAT!

ACCORDING TO THE RULES, THE FIGHT MAY GO ON UNTIL SUNRISE TOMORROW. THE LOSER IS THE MAN WHO STAYS DOWN AFTER A COUNT OF 100! OFF YOU GO, AND MAY THE BEST MAN WIN THE PRIZE!

BONK!

CLONK!

V SESTERTII ON CLEVERDIX!
X ON MAJESTIX!
XV ON CLEVERDIX!
41A

S EVENING COMES ON, MANY OF THE AUDIENCE,
RING OF THE SHOW, LEAVE THE RING
THEY OUGHT TO REVISE THE RULES OF THESE PRIZEFIGHTS.
PAF!
PAF!

IT'S LATE. I'M GOING TO BED, ASTERIX!
YAAAWN! SO ARE WE, DOGMATIX AND I DON'T TAKE MUCH INTEREST IN FIGHTS WHEN THERE AREN'T ANY ROMANS OR ANY BOARS.
ZZZZ

EN ASTERIX IS UNABLE
KEEP HIS EYES OPEN.
. ALONE, IN THE MOON-
GHT, THE TWO CHIEFS
E STILL EQUALLY MATCHED.
PAF!
PAF!
BZZZZZ!

AND AT SUNRISE...
COCKADOODLE-DO!

?!?
RRRRR!
ZZZZ!
41B

FRIENDS, FATE HAS DECIDED THE RESULT OF THE SINGLE COMBAT... NO ONE HAS WON AND NO ONE HAS LOST!

BUT YOU CAN HAVE A YOUNG, STRONG CHIEF IF YOU CHOOSE HISTRIONIX TO LEAD YOU, AND MELODRAMA WILL MAKE A WISE AND BEAUTIFUL CHIEF'S WIFE!
HURRAH! LONG LIVE HISTRIONIX! LONG LIVE MELODRAMA!

?!?

OH WELL, I RATHER THINK ALL WE CAN DO IS GET DRESSED AGAIN!
YOU SAID IT, FAT-FACE!

REUNITED AT LAST, UNDER THE RULE OF THEIR NEW CHIEF HISTRIONIX, THE GAULS OF THE VILLAGE DIVERT PART OF THE NEARBY RIVER INTO THE DITCH, WHICH NO LONGER SERVES ANY USEFUL PURPOSE. AND NOW THERE IS NO PARTY OF THE RIGHT OR PARTY OF THE LEFT, ONLY A RIGHT BANK AND A LEFT BANK, RUNNING WATER ON EVERYONE'S DOOR-STEP AND FREEDOM FOR ALL THE VILLAGERS TO GO TO AND FRO.

THE CHILDREN CAN STILL GATHER THE FRUITS OF OTHER PEOPLE'S LABOURS WITH IMPUNITY...

YOU'VE GOT NO RIGHT TO DO THAT! THAT'S MY TREE!!!
SCRUNCH!

NEW AND PRACTICAL USE IS FOUND
OR THE TWO GATEWAYS OF THE VILLAGE.
ERE YOU SEE THE FIRST ONE-WAY
YSTEM KNOWN TO ANCIENT HISTORY.

AND SCHIZOPHRENIX'S HUT IS REBUILT AT LAST... THOUGH THE ARCHITECTS DID SLIP UP HERE AND THERE IN THEIR PLANS.
SPLOSH!

ANY IDEA WHAT BECAME OF THAT SCOUNDREL CODFIX?
NO, BUT I SHOULD BE SURPRISED IF HE WAS STILL UP TO DIRTY WORK.

SURE ENOUGH, IN THE ROMAN CAMP...
WELL, SLAVE, HAVE YOU DONE THOSE VEGETABLES YET?
AND THE LAUNDRY? AND DON'T FORGET THE IRONING!

HE WEDDING OF MELODRAMA AND HISTRIONIX
S CELEBRATED AMIDST REJOICINGS FOR ALL
ND BOARS FOR SOME.
SCRUNCH! SCRUNCH!
SCRUNCH SCRUNCH

E TIME
OMES TO SAY
OODBYE.
HOW CAN WE EVER THANK YOU FOR ALL WE OWE YOU?
YOU'RE HAPPY, AND THAT'S ALL THE THANKS WE NEED!

HUH!

LOOK HERE, OBELIX, IT'S THREE DAYS SINCE WE LEFT OUR FRIENDS' VILLAGE, AND YOU HAVEN'T UTTERED A SINGLE WORD! WHAT'S THE MATTER?

BOOHOOHOO! I GET UPSET BY LOVE STORIES WITH HAPPY ENDINGS TOO!
!?!
HUH!

HOWEVER, THE PLEASURES OF HOME-COMING OVERSHADOW ALL OTHER EMOTIONS.
HOW NICE TO BE BACK IN THE CALM AND PEACEFUL ATMOSPHERE OF OUR OWN VILLAGE!
YES, I CAN ALREADY SMELL BOARS ROASTING ON THE SPIT FOR US!
WOOF!

SPLATCH!

AND FOR THE XXVTH TIME, UNDER THE STARRY SKY RULED BY THE GOD TOUTATIS, THE PEOPLE OF ASTERIX'S VILLAGE HAPPILY CELEBRATE THE RETURN OF THEIR HEROES WITH THE TRADITIONAL AND INDISPENSABLE BANQUET.
ALL THAT ABOUT THE GREAT DIVIDE REALLY DOES SOUND MOST IMPROBABLE!
YES... IT WAS SO RIDICULOUS I DARE SAY FUTURE GENERATIONS WILL NEVER BELIEVE A WORD OF IT!
TU-WHOO
SCRUNCH! SCRUNCH!
SCROTCH!
THE END
-UDERZO- 4.80

R. GOSCINNY Asterix A. UDERZO

Asterix AND THE BLACK GOLD

Written and illustrated by Albert UDERZO

GOSCINNY AND UDERZO

PRESENT

An Asterix Adventure

ASTERIX AND THE BLACK GOLD

Written and Illustrated by ALBERT UDERZO

Translated by Anthea Bell *and* Derek Hockridge

Orion
Children's Books

à René

IN THE QUIET, PEACEFUL DEPTHS OF THE GAULISH FOREST, EVERYTHING SEEMS TO INDICATE THAT IT IS DINNER TIME...
TAP TAP TAP TAP TAP TAP
SCRUNCH SCRUNCH

BUT SOME OF THE FOREST WELLERS HAVE LOST THEIR PPETITES.
OINK! RUNT! OINK! OINK!
GRUNT! OINK! OINK OINK!
MUNCH! MUNCH!

(AUTHOR'S NOTE: WITH APOLOGIES TO PURISTS, WE PROVIDE A DUBBED VERSION TO FACILITATE YOUR UNDERSTANDING OF THE DIALOGUE.)
ARE YOU QUITE SURE WE AREN'T GOING TO MEET ANY OF THOSE CRAZY GAULS FROM THE VILLAGE?
I TOLD YOU, YOU'RE QUITE SAFE WITH ME. WHY ARE YOU SCARED?
MUNCH! MUNCH!

BECAUSE THEY'VE WOLFED DOWN, SCRUNCHED, CRUNCHED AND GOBBLED UP MY WHOLE HERD, AND I AM THE SOLE SURVIVOR OF A LARGE FAMILY, THAT'S WHY!!!

CALM DOWN! NO NEED TO GO RANTING LIKE A BARNSTORMER*! I ADMIT THEY'RE GOOD AT BRINGING HOME THE BACON...
*HAM ACTOR

...BUT AS WHAT MUST BE CURED CAN'T BE ENDURED, I'VE WORKED OUT AN INFALLIBLE SYSTEM! I'LL BET YOU WE NEVER FEATURE ON THE GAUL'S MENU!
AND WHO WINS IF YOU LOSE YOUR BET?

CRAZY GAULS!
DINNER!

QUICK! FOLLOW ME! I TELL YOU, IT'LL BE A MIRACLE IF THEY GET US!
HUH! PIGS MIGHT FLY!

GRUNT! IF I EVER GET OUT OF THIS, I SWEAR I'LL NEVER BE DISGRUNTLED WITH MY LOT AGAIN!

EEK! THIS ONE'S PERSISTENT AS WELL AS BRAWNY*!
*PIG-HEADED
HANG ON, WE'RE NEARLY THERE!
SNIFF

CRAZY GAULS!
ROMANS!

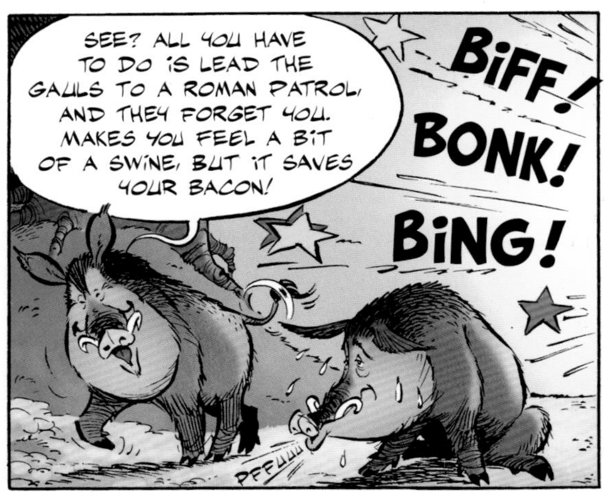
SEE? ALL YOU HAVE TO DO IS LEAD THE GAULS TO A ROMAN PATROL, AND THEY FORGET YOU. MAKES YOU FEEL A BIT OF A SWINE, BUT IT SAVES YOUR BACON!
BIFF!
BONK!
BING!
PFFUUU

AND SO, A LITTLE LATER, IN THE ROMAN CAMP OF COMPENDIUM...
...AND WHAT'S MORE, THEY'VE TRAINED WILD BOAR TO LEAD THEM STRAIGHT TO OUR PATROLS!!!
WE CAN'T HAVE THIS! CAESAR MUST BE INFORMED!

IN ROME...
NO, WE MOST CERTAINLY CAN'T HAVE THIS!!!

THAT ARMORICAN VILLAGE IS STILL HOLDING THE MIGHT OF ROME UP TO RIDICULE!

AND I HEAR THAT MY LEGIONS NOW HAVE TO FACE HORDES OF WILD BEASTS!

THE MORALE OF MY TROOPS IS AT ROCK BOTTOM, AND I AM THE LAUGHING STOCK OF MY ENEMIES IN THE SENATE!
AS WE ALL KNOW, WE HAVE FAILED TO CONQUER THOSE INDOMITABLE GAULS BY FORCE, CORRUPTION, OR EVEN KIDNAPPING, AND YET...
3A

M. DEVIUS SURREPTITIUS, YOU'RE CHIEF OF MY SECRET SERVICE, M.I.VI. IF YOU HAVE AN IDEA, BY JUPITER, LET'S HEAR IT!
O CAESAR, THE SECRETS OF THE DRUIDS ARE PASSED ON ONLY FROM DRUID TO DRUID BY WORD OF MOUTH!

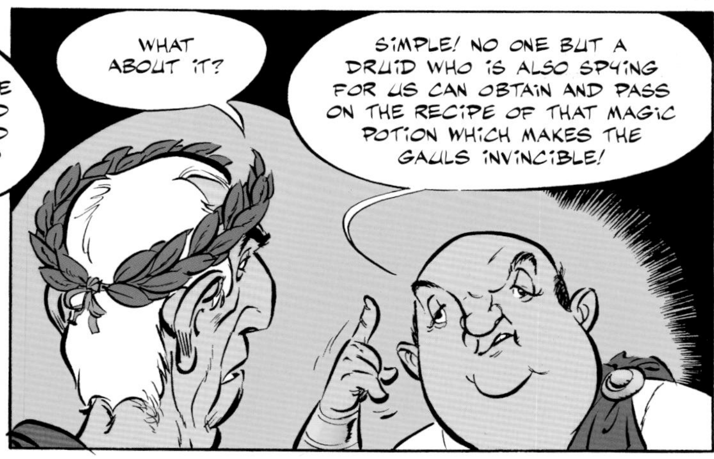
WHAT ABOUT IT?
SIMPLE! NO ONE BUT A DRUID WHO IS ALSO SPYING FOR US CAN OBTAIN AND PASS ON THE RECIPE OF THAT MAGIC POTION WHICH MAKES THE GAULS INVINCIBLE!

AND AMONG MY AGENTS I HAVE JUST SUCH A DRUID!
THEN WHAT ARE YOU WAITING FOR? FETCH HIM!

HE'S ALREADY HERE, CAESAR, QUITE CLOSE TO YOU!
?!?
YOU CAN COME DOWN FROM YOUR PEDESTAL NOW, DUBBELOSIX!
3B

*HAIL CAESAR, THOSE ABOUT TO GET RICH QUI[CKLY] SALUTE YOU.

*THE EARLIEST KNOWN USE OF A BUG IN ESPIONAGE.

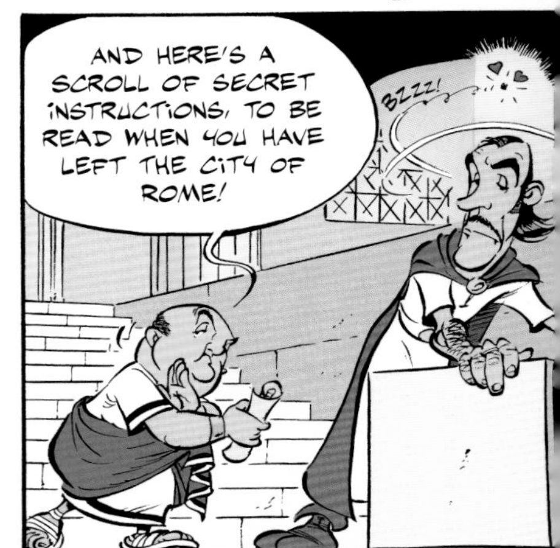

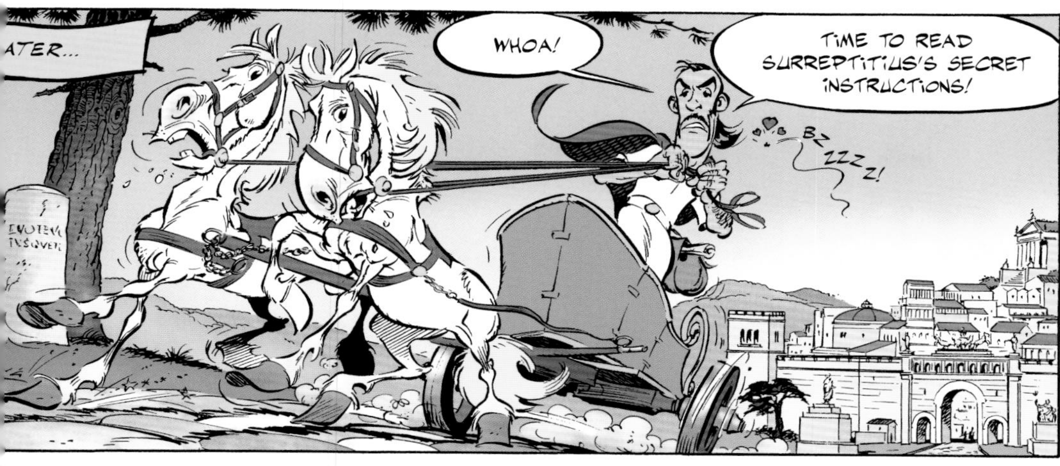

ATER...
WHOA!
TIME TO READ SURREPTITIUS'S SECRET INSTRUCTIONS!
BZ ZZZZ!

WHY RENDER UNTO CAESAR WHAT WE CAN KEEP FOR OURSELVES? THE MAGIC POTION WILL MAKE US INVINCIBLE, AND LIKE A DOUBLE-HEADED EAGLE, WE CAN RULE THE WHOLE ROMAN EMPIRE.
M. DEVIUS SURREPTITIUS
P.S. AFTER YOU HAVE READ THIS THE PAPYRUS WILL AUTO-DESTRUCT.

?!
PSSCHCHCH...

HO, HO! CAESAR AND SURREPTITIUS ARE A COUPLE OF FOOLS! I PLAN TO BE A VULTURE RULING THE GALLO-ROMAN EMPIRE ALONE!
BZZZZ
KISS!

OH LEAVE ME ALONE, YOU WRETCHED CREATURE!
BZZZZZZ
5A

MEANWHILE, ON THE ARMORICAN COAST, ALL IS PEACEFUL IN THE LITTLE GAULISH VILLAGE WHERE ASTERIX AND HIS FRIENDS LIVE.

IT'S A FUNNY THING, BUT WHEN WE GO WILD BOAR-HUNTING THESE DAYS WE KEEP FINDING ROMAN PATROLS!
YES, YOU'D THINK THEY'D KNOW BY NOW BOAR IS ONE OF OUR SACRED COWS! SCRUNCH!

AND YOU CERTAINLY GO THE WHOLE HOG EATING IT!
SCRUNCH! MUNCH! SCRUNCH!
5B

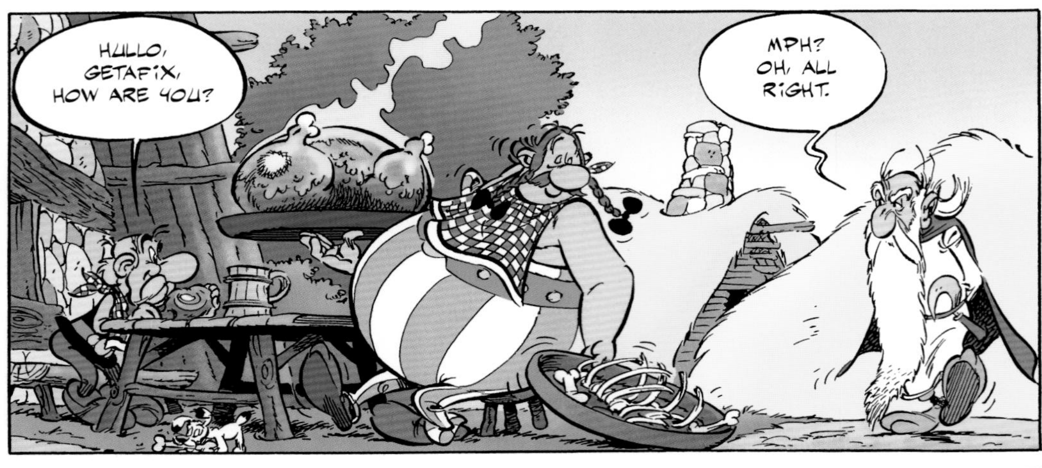

IF GETAFIX HAS A PROBLEM, WE MUST HELP HIM! ASTERIX, YOU FOLLOW HIM DISCREETLY. YOU MAY FIND OUT THE REASON FOR HIS STRANGE BEHAVIOUR!

IT WILL BE TERRIBLE IF HE DOESN'T COME, TERRIBLE!
7A

APPALLING!

GHASTLY!

CATASTROPHIC!
SLAM!

...AND THEN HE SAID, 'APPALLING! GHASTLY! CATASTROPHIC!'
IF GETAFIX IS ALL THAT WORRIED, THE SKY MUST BE ABOUT TO FALL ON OUR HEADS!!!

SO FAR, HOWEVER, NOTHING BUT NIGHT HAS FALLEN ON THE VILLAGE AND ITS PEOPLE, SOME OF WHOM ARE IN FOR TROUBLED DREAMS.
7B

BUT NEXT MORNING...
COME QUICKLY! EKONOMIKRISIS THE PHOENICIAN MERCHANT HAS LANDED ON THE BEACH!!!

HE'S HERE! AT LAST!!

HULLO, ASTERIX! NICE DAY ISN'T IT?
?!

I WOULDN'T MIND TASTING YOUR NEW BARREL OF BEER, VITALSTATISTIX! DON'T FORGET!
?!

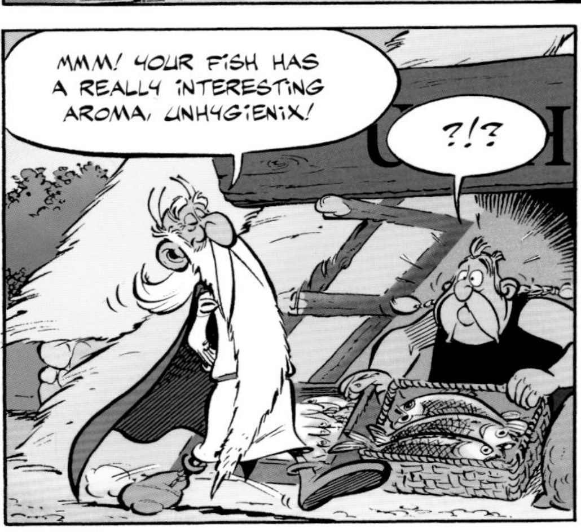

MMM! YOUR FISH HAS A REALLY INTERESTING AROMA, UNHYGIENIX!
?!?

SO GETAFIX WAS WAITING FOR EKONOMIKRISIS AND HIS CARGO!
AND HE APPRECIATED MY FISH, SO THERE!
THAT'S WHAT WORRIES ME. ANYONE IN THAT STATE MUST BE ON THE BRINK OF SUICIDE!

HERE YOU ARE AT LAST, EKONOMIKRISIS, OLD CHAP!
HULLO THERE, GETAFIX! I'VE BEEN LOOKING FORWARD TO SEEING YOU ALL AGAIN EVER SINCE MY LAST VOYAGE! LOOK WHAT I'VE BROUGHT FROM TYRE, SPECIALLY FOR YOU!

AND OF COURSE YOU'VE BROUGHT WHAT I ORDERED WHEN YOU LAST PUT IN HERE?
REMIND ME WHAT IT WAS, WILL YOU?

ROCK OIL, OF COURSE!
BY THE GREAT GOD BAAL! I KNEW I'D FORGOTTEN SOMETHING!!!
SLAP!

WHAAAT?
NOW DON'T GET WORKED UP! I CAN LET YOU HAVE PURPLE, INCENSE, SPICES, PRECIOUS STONES...

NOOO! I WANT ROCK OIL! I ABSOLUTELY MUST HAVE...
THUMP! THUMP! THUMP! THUMP!

AAARRGH!

BOING!

IT'S A STROKE. I'VE SEEN THIS BEFORE. MY BROTHER-IN-LAW HAD ONE WHEN THE ROMAN QUAESTOR SENT HIM HIS TAX DEMAND!
QUICK, OBELIX, LET'S CARRY HIM TO HIS HUT!

I'M SO SORRY! BUT WHY WOULD ANYONE GET INTO SUCH A STATE OVER COMMON ROCK OIL?
WHAT'S ROCK OIL?

OIL WHICH GUSHES OUT OF ROCKY GROUND, HENCE ITS NAME. IT'S FOUND MAINLY IN MESOPOTAMIA, AND IS ALSO CALLED NAPHTHA.

AND WHAT'S SO SPECIAL ABOUT THIS OIL?
NOTHING! YOU CAN BURN IT IN AN OIL LAMP, BUT IT SMELLS SO BAD NO ONE USES IT MUCH.

I'M WORRIED! HE DOESN'T SEEM TO BE IMPROVING, AND WE CAN'T DOSE HIM WITH MAGIC POTION BECAUSE WE'VE RUN OUT. GO AND LOOK FOR ANOTHER DRUID TO TREAT HIM, ASTERIX!

HE'LL NEED VINEGAR TOO FOR A GAULISH DRESSING.
GETAFIX IS NO LONGER IN HIS SALAD DAYS. WE MUST GET HELP FOR HIM, QUICK!
GRRRR!

?
?!
BZZZ!
WOOF!
WOOF!

HEEL, DOGMATIX! HEEL!
WHO ARE YOU, WHERE DO YOU COME FROM, WHAT ARE YOU DOING?
MY NAME IS DUBBELOSIX, AND I AM A WANDERING DRUID. I COME FROM NOWHERE IN PARTICULAR, AND I OFFER MY KNOWLEDGE AND SERVICES TO THOSE WHO NEED THEM.
BZZZ
GRRR

CAN YOU CURE A DRUID WHO SLIPPED ON AN OILY ROCK?
?!? NOT A VERY COMMON ACCIDEN BUT I THINK I COULD COPE!
BZZZZ!
GRRRR!

WHAT LUCK WE MET YOU! OUR DRUID GETAFIX IS ILL AND NEEDS OUR CARE!
WHAT LUCK I MET THEM! AND THEIR DRUID NEEDS MY CARE, TOO!

HALT!!! THIS IS A CHECK-POINT!
GOODY! A ROMAN ROAD BLOCK!
OH NO! THESE FOOLS WILL RUIN THINGS!
THERE'S NO TIME TO PLA AROUND, OBELI GETAFIX IS WAITING!

DON'T BE FRIGHTENED! I'LL FIX THIS!
?
CLANG!

HUH! US, FRIGHTENED?
BZZZZ!

FOLLOW THEM!

BZZZZ
FRIGHTENED? THIS DRUID IS CRAZY!

PSCHHH!

BANG!
BING!
EEEK!
CLONG!
OUCH!
MUMMY!

JOIN THE LIGHT CAVALRY, THEY SAID...
WE SHOULD HAVE SHOWN MORE HORSE SENSE!
YOU SAID IT! STRAIGHT FROM THE HORSE'S MOUTH!
MY CHEST FEELS A LITTLE HOARSE...

DON'T GET ON YOUR HIGH HORSE! THEY CAN'T GO FAR! THEY'RE MAKING STRAIGHT FOR THE CLIFF, SO THEY'LL SOON BE HORS DE COMBAT!

WE'VE THROWN THEM OFF NOW!
BZZZ!
WATCH OUT! THE CLIFF!

BZZZZ!
FRIGHTENED OF WHAT, MAY I ASK?

DON'T BE FRIGHTENED! IT'S ALL TAKEN CARE OF!
HIS INSINUATIONS ARE GETTING ME DOWN!
BZZZZZZ!
CLICK!

?
SPLOSH!

SOMETHING SHOULD HAVE HAPPENED WHEN I PRESSED THAT BUTTON!!!
BZZZ

SOON AFTERWARDS...
WELL, WE WERE MORE FRIGHTENED THAN HURT!
BZZZ

HEY YOU, HOLD YOUR HORSES!!! NOW JUST LISTEN HERE, YOU!!!
?!

YOUR FRIEND QUITE FRIGHTENS ME SOMETIMES!
HE'S A BIT TOUCHY, BUT HE'S GOT A HEART OF GOLD!
BZZZ

I'M REALLY WORRIED! GETAFIX HASN'T COME ROUND YET!
THIS IS THE TONIC HE NEEDS TO BUCK HIM UP!
BZZZ

BZZZZ!
GLUG! GLUG! GLUG!

AARGH! SPLUTTER! CHOKE!

HIC!

A'SH GOOD! WHAT... HIC! WHAT ISH IT?
A GRAIN SPIRIT CALLED CALEDONIAN! *
BZZZ
*ANCIENT SCOTCH

BUT IT MAY BE A BIT STRONG NEAT... I THINK IT MIGHT BE BETTER DILUTED WITH A SPOT OF SODA!
BZZZ!

O, YE'LL TAK' ... THE HIC! ... HIGH ROAD...
13A

... AND, I'LL TAK' THE LOW... HIC! ...ROAD...
OH, WELL DONE! HE'S BACK ON HIS FEET AGAIN, BUT OFF HIS HEAD!
BZZZ

...AND I'LL BE IN CALEDONIA AFORE YE... THA'SH THE SHPIRIT!
?

OWEVER, GETAFIX S SOON IN LOW SPIRITS AGAIN.
YOU WANT TO KNOW WHY I THINK ROCK OIL IS SO IMPORTANT? IT'S LIQUID GOLD! WITHOUT ROCK OIL...
BZZZ

... KNOWN TO THE ROMANS AS PETRA OLEUM, WE SHALL HAVE NO MORE MAGIC POTION!
?
13B

HUH! WE'VE BEEN IN WORSE TROUBLE BEFORE! WITH OUR CHIEF'S PERMISSION, I'LL GO TO MESOPOTAMIA AND BRING SOME ROCK OIL BACK!

EKONOMIKRISIS, CAN YOU TAKE US TO FIND ROCK OIL?
NOT UNTIL I'VE SOLD OFF MY STOCK, ASTERIX.

OBELIX AND I WILL SELL YOUR STOCK ON THE WAY!
ALL RIGHT, THEN!

GETAFIX, I AM A DRUID TOO! WOULD YOU GIVE ME THE RECIPE FOR THE MAGIC POTION?
BZZZ
HMM... WHAT WOULD YOU DO WITH IT?

OH, JUST HELP THE WEAK AND THE OPPRESSED A BIT!
MAYBE... IF I CAN'T GET HOLD OF ALL THE INGREDIENTS FOR THE RECIPE...
ZZZZ!

...BUT I'M SURE ASTERIX WILL BRING ME BACK SOME ROCK OIL!
SO I MUST MAKE SURE ASTERIX'S MISSION FAILS!!!
BZZZ!

YOU'RE QUITE RIGHT, GETAFIX! I SHOULD LIKE TO CONTRIBUTE TO THE SUCCESS OF THIS VENTURE MYSELF! IF NO ONE MINDS, I'LL GO TO MESOPOTAMIA WITH ASTERIX AND OBELIX!
BZZZ
15A

E DAY OF PARTURE MES.
AND REMEMBER THE FATE OF THE VILLAGE IS IN YOUR HANDS! WITHOUT POTION, WE HAVEN'T GOT A LEG TO STAND ON!
OR A SHIELD, FATTY!
HERE, ASTERIX! LUCKILY I KEPT THIS GOURD OF MAGIC POTION IN RESERVE!

AND KEEP AN EYE ON DUBBELOSIX! SOMETHING TELLS ME NOT TO TRUST HIM!
DON'T WORRY, I'LL WATCH HIM!

I WILL NOW GIVE YOU...
YOU JUST TRY IT!
BUT WHERE'S DUBBELOSIX?
15B

NOW, TAKE MY MESSAGE TO SURREPTITIUS!

NO DAWDLING ON THE WAY! IT'S URGENT!
BZZZZ

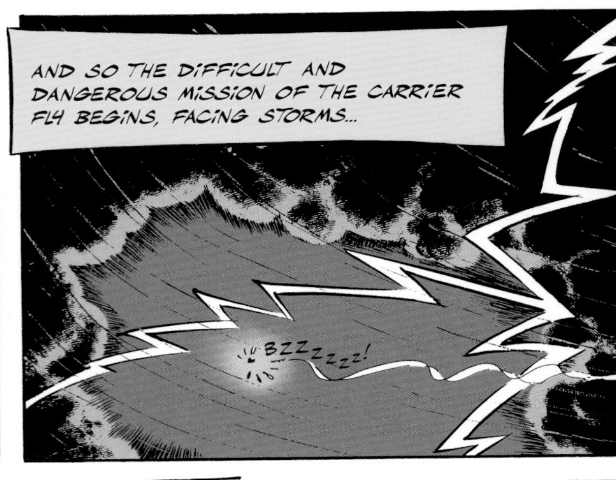
AND SO THE DIFFICULT AND DANGEROUS MISSION OF THE CARRIER FLY BEGINS, FACING STORMS...
BZZZZZZ!

...AND MANY OTHER PERILS...
?!
BZZZZ!

ZIP!
ZIP!
ZIP!
ZIP!
SNAP!

...THE SMALLEST MEMBER OF CAESAR'S SECRET SERVICE FINALLY REACHES HER JOURNEY'S END, WORN OUT.
?!
FLOP!

YUK! A FLY IN MY SOUP!! HOW REVOLTING!!!

EUGGH!
WHY WAS I IN THE SOUP? WHAT'S BUGGING HIM?
PLOP!

LET'S SEE WHAT DUBBELOSIX HAS TO SAY. 'AM ON PHOENICIAN SHIP BOUND FOR MESOPOTAMIA, WITH INDOMITABLE GAULS. AT ALL COSTS PREVENT LANDING.'

WELL, DUBBELOSIX MUST HAVE HIS REASONS. I'LL GO AND GIVE THE NECESSARY ORDERS!

AND YOU FLY STRAIGHT BACK TO DUBBELOSIX! SHOO!
TAKE IT EASY! YOU MAY FIND I'M A FLY IN THE OINTMENT!
POC!

MEANWHILE, SAILING THE HIGH SEAS...
IT'S A FUNNY THING, ASTERIX, DUBBELOSIX HASN'T BEEN ATTRACTING INSECTS LATELY!
NO, I FANCY THERE ARE NO FLIES ON HIM.

MORE PARTNERS IN YOUR COMPANY WHO FAILED TO READ THEIR CONTRACTS BEFORE SIGNING?*
NO, I'VE STARTED UP A PACKAGE HOLIDAY BUSINESS. THESE ARE HOLIDAYMAKERS AND I'M THEIR TOUR OPERATOR. I'M A PRETTY SHARP OPERATOR TOO!
* SEE ASTERIX THE GLADIATOR

SAIL AHOY, MR OPERATOR!
CUSTOMERS! QUICK, HOIST THE FLAG!

SPECIAL BARGAIN FORTNIGHT

MR OPERATOR, THE CUSTOMERS ARE HOISTING A BLACK FLAG IN REPLY!
?!

IT'S THE PIRATES! THEY'LL TAKE ALL MY MERCHANDISE!
COME TO THINK OF IT, WHY NOT?
17A

SHIVER ME TIMBERS, ME HEARTIES! THE CARGO OF THAT PHOENICIAN SHIP WILL MAKE OUR FORTUNES! HO, HO, HO!
TEE HEEHEE!

ER... HOLIDAYMAKERS, DO YOU KNOW AN EXCITING NEW GAME CALLED NAVAL BATTLES?
NO, MR OPERATOR, AND WE'RE SICK AND TIRED OF YOUR HOLIDAY ENTERTAINMENTS! WE WANT TO GO HOME AS SOON AS POSSIBLE AND GET BACK TO WORK FOR A BIT OF A REST!

I DON'T THINK WE CAN COUNT ON THE HOLIDAYMAKERS' SENSE OF FUN, OBELIX!
GOODY! THE FEWER CRAZY ONES AROUND THE MORE MAD FUN!

YOOHOO!
THE CRAZY GAULS!
17B

THEY SEEM A BIT SOFT, ASTERIX, IN SPITE OF THE BRACING SEA BREEZES!
YES, THEY'RE ALL AT SEA, OBELIX!
BOING!
SMACK!

BY ESUS! WE'LL HAVE OUR WORK CUT OUT TO STOP THOSE TW LANDING SAFELY!

WELL, HOLIDAYMAKERS, DIDN'T I PROMISE YOU GOOD CLEAN FUN ON THIS VOYAGE?
IT'S THE FUNNIEST THING I EVER SAW!
YES, A PITCHED SEA BATTLE ISN'T A BAD NOTION!

SOON AFTERWARDS...
PLEASE SPARE MY SHIP! I HAVEN'T FINISHED PAYING FOR HER YET!
GRRR!

DO WE SINK HER AND MAKE SAIL, ASTERIX?
NO, WE DON'T SINK HER, WE MAKE A SAL OBELIX! YOU'D LIKE TO BUY UP OUR ENTIRE STOCK, WOULDN YOU?
WHO, ME?

ONE THOUSAND NINE HUNDRED AND NINETY-NINE... TWO THOUSAND. THAT'S IT!

YOU'VE RUINED ME! HOW WILL I PAY THE LAST THREE INSTALMENTS ON MY SHIP?
RE-SELL OUR MERCHANDISE, OF COURSE!

NON OMNIA POSSUMUS OMNES!
WELL? I SAVED THE SHIP, DIDN'T I?
WHATEVER HE MEANS, I VOTE WE PLAY POSSUM NEXT TIME!
WELL DONE, FRIENDS! AS SALESMEN, YOU CERTAINLY PACK PLENTY OF PUNCH!
THEY SHOULD WIN A FREE HOLIDAY!
I JUST HOPE THE ROMANS CA DO BETTER THA THOSE FOOLS!

D JUST THEN...
SAIL AHOY, MR OPERATOR!

...A ROMAN GALLEY SAILS INTO THEIR KEN.
PHOENICIAN SHIP AHEAD!
IT MUST BE THE ONE CARRYING THOSE INDOMITABLE GAULS WE HEARD ABOUT!

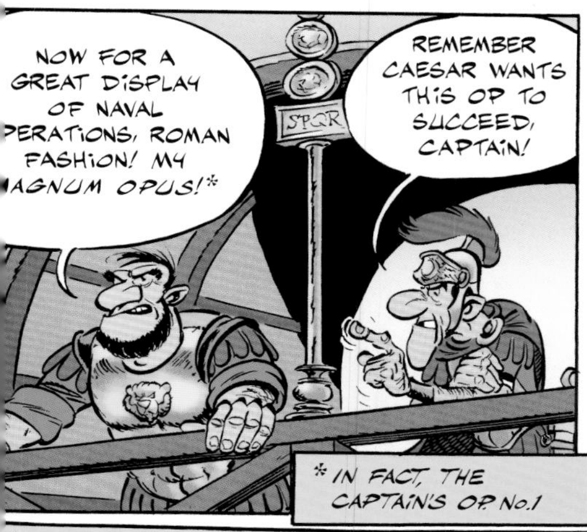
NOW FOR A GREAT DISPLAY OF NAVAL PERATIONS, ROMAN FASHION! MY AGNUM OPUS!*
REMEMBER CAESAR WANTS THIS OP TO SUCCEED, CAPTAIN!
SPQR
* IN FACT, THE CAPTAIN'S OP. No.1

GOODY! ROMANS! NOW FOR SOME FUN AT LAST!
SOMETHING TELLS ME THEY'RE NOT HERE FOR FUN!
THE FLY HAS DELIVERED MY MESSAGE ALL RIGHT! WELL DONE THE SECRET SERVICE!
CLAP! CLAP! CLAP!
19A

NOW HAVE A CHANCE TO OBSERVE THE SUPERBLY FICIENT BOARDING TACTICS PRACTISED BY THE ROMAN Y. FIRST, BALLISTAE THROW OUT GRAPPLING HOOKS...
WHOOSH!
WHOOSH!

THE ROMANS SIMPLY PULL, THE ENEMY'S FAT IS IN THE !
WHAT DO YOU MEAN, THE ENEMY'S FAT?
WHOOOOSHHH...
BOING!
19B

SHALL WE GET THEM, OBELIX?
LET'S GET THEM, ASTERIX!
GLUG! GLUG!

BOARD 'EM!

YOU CAN'T DO THAT! THAT'S A FOUL!
WE ARE BOARDING YOU, SEE?

PIF
PAF!

ALWAYS THE SAME OLD STORY: AS SOON AS THEY FEEL THEY'RE OUTNUMBERED THE ROMANS WON'T PLAY!
FAREWELL AND ADIEU TO YOU BOLD ROMAN SOLDIERS, FAREWELL AND ADIEU TO YOU SOLDIERS OF ROME...
BONG!
BAM!
FLAP!
GRRRR!

WHAT A SHAME I'VE GOT NOTHING LEFT TO SELL!
THESE WATER SPOR REALLY PEF THINGS UP

IT'S NOT TRUE! IT JUST ISN'T TRUE!!!

BUT IT IS! AND SOON AFTERWARDS...
SAID IT WAS HIS MAGNUM OPUS, THE FOOL!
GLUG! GLUG! GLUG! GLUG!
I FEAR THAT WA MY NAVAL OP. No. AND LAST!

D
CE AGAIN...
OMAN GALLEY
AHOY,
R OPERATOR.

...THE NOW CLASSIC
BOARDING TACTICS...
BONG!

RE FOLLOWED
AN EQUALLY
ADITIONAL
GHT AND ITS
TERMATH.
WE'RE
HAVING FUN,
AREN'T WE,
ASTERIX?
YES, BUT IT
SEEMS ODD FOR
THE ROMANS TO
BE SO KEEN ON
FIGHTING US,
OBELIX!
BANG!
BING!
BIFF!
PAF!

EVERY TIME I SEE IT
AGAIN I FIND SOMETHING
ELSE TO APPRECIATE!
21A

T IN ROME...
BY JUPITER,
THEY SHALL FEEL THE
ANGER OF CAESAR! I'LL
HAVE ALL THE
MEDITERRANEAN PORTS
BLOCKADED!

AND LOOK SHARP!
I DON'T EXPECT MY NAVAL
COMMANDERS TO STOP AND
CONTEMPLATE ANY NAVELS!*
*POPULAR MEDITERRANEAN FRUIT

I WANT TO MAKE SURE
NOT EVEN A FLY COULD GET
THROUGH THE NET!
HM... AND
THINKING OF
FLIES...

SURREPTITIUS!

ANY NEWS OF YOUR AGENT
DUBBEL... DUBBEL
SOMETHING?
SNAP
I'M AFRAID WE HAVE
A COMMUNICATIONS
PROBLEM, O CAESAR!
21B

PROBLEM? WHAT SORT OF PROBLEM?
OUR CARRIER FLY IS GOING SLOW, AND IF SHE ACTUALLY GOES ON STRIKE...

WELL, IF IT'S WILDLIFE WE'RE DISCUSSING, HOW WOULD YOU LIKE TO FIND OUT IF THE LIONS IN THE CIRCUS ARE ON HUNGER STRIKE?!!!
BONK

I MUST TRY TO ENTICE HER BACK...
WHERE'S A PRETTY FLY, THEN...?
Honey

BZZZ ZZ ZZZ ZZZZ
I MIGHT HAVE KNOWN IT!
BZZZZZzzz
ZZZZZZZzzz
Honey

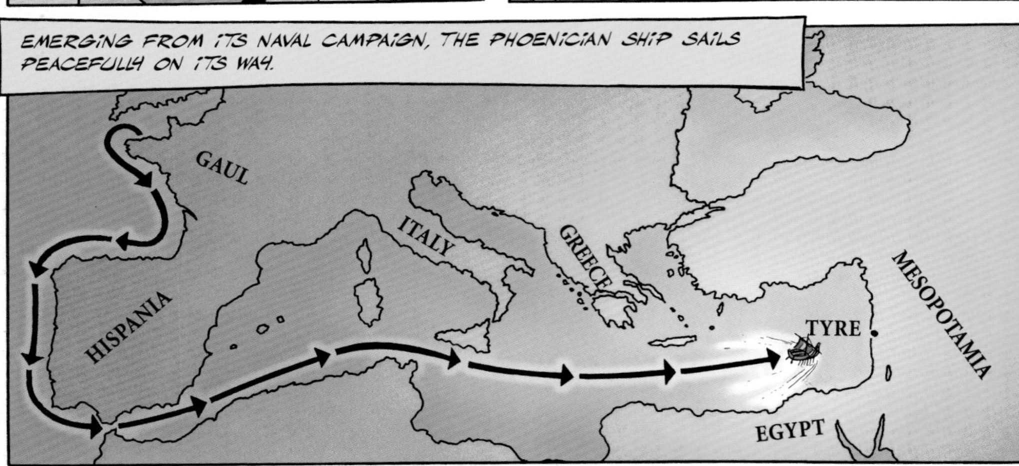
EMERGING FROM ITS NAVAL CAMPAIGN, THE PHOENICIAN SHIP SAILS PEACEFULLY ON ITS WAY.
GAUL
ITALY
GREECE
HISPANIA
TYRE
MESOPOTAMIA
EGYPT

ASTERIX, I'M TIRED OF THIS VOYAGE, AND I GET HUNGRY WHEN I'M TIRED!
WAIT A BIT LONGER, OBELIX. WE SHOULD SOON BE LANDING AT TYRE!

DON'T TIRE NOW, HERE COMES TYRE!

BUT ONE OF THE FINEST OF PHOENICIAN TRADING PORTS HAS BECOME INACCESSIBLE. THE HARBOUR MOUTH IS BLOCKED BY BIREMES, TRIREMES, QUADRIREMES AND QUINQUIREMES.

I'VE NEVER SEEN SO MANY WARSHIPS BEFORE! WHAT'S IT ALL IN AID OF?
I RATHER THINK WE'RE GOING TO FIND OUT!

SURE ENOUGH...
?!
PLOP!
PLOP!
PLOP!

ALL HANDS TO THE OARS! FULL SPEED ASTERN!
PLOP!
PLOP!

TEEHEE! JULIUS CAESAR'S NOT SUCH A SILLY OLD GEEZER!
WELL, WE CAN ALWAYS LAND AT SIDON, BYBLOS OR ARAD WITH A LITTLE CRAFT!*
*BUT NOT A BIG GALLEY...
23A

OR OUTSIDE SIDON...

...BYBLOS...

...AND ARAD, THINGS ARE JUST THE SAME...

I'M HUNGRY, ASTERIX!
THAT'S A PITY. WE HAD JUST ENOUGH PROVISIONS TO LAST US TO TYRE, AND NOW THEY'RE ALL GONE!

ALL THE COOK COULD PRODUCE IS SOUP!
I CALL THIS OMINOUS.
WHO'S THIS OMINUS? YOUR COOK?
23B

I'M SURE OF IT NOW: THE ROMANS HAVE BEEN WARNED. THEY KNOW WHAT WE'RE AFTER!

ER... BUT HOW COULD THAT BE? WE ARE THE ONLY ONES WHO...
SPLOSH!

OH NO! I CAN'T STAND FLIES IN MY SOUP!!!

?!? BUT... IT'S THE BUG!

YOU CAN SEE WE'RE GETTING NEAR THE COAST; HE'S ATTRACTING THEM AGAIN!

ER... NO... THE FACT IS, I JUST LOVE TO HELP POOR LITTLE FLIES, AND THIS ONE NEEDS MY ATTENTION, SO IF YOU DON'T MIND...
?!
?!
?!

THAT DRUID IS CRAZY!
HOWEVER, HE WOULDN'T HURT A FLY!
TAP! TAP!
GLUG! GLUG!

GET A MOVE ON. CAESAR IS WAITING, AND SO ARE THE LIONS.
M. DEVIUS SURREPTITIUS

I'M SURE THE GAULS WON'T GIVE UP AT THIS POINT! I'LL TELL CAESAR TO HAVE ALL STOCKS OF ROCK OIL IN PALESTINE DESTROYED!
SLURP! SLURP! SLURP!

PHEW! THAT'S BETTER! THE WORST OF THESE LONG-DISTANCE FLIGHTS IS THE JET-LAG!
Honey

BE QUICK! SUCCESS AND MY FORTUNE DEPEND ON YOU!
TO THINK I'M STUCK WITH LOVING HIM! MEN ARE SO INCONSIDERATE!

WE'RE VERY SORRY TO HAVE CAUSED YOU SO MANY PROBLEMS, EKONOMIKRISIS!
OH, I RATHER LIKE COCKING A SNOOK AT THE ROMANS!

ANYWAY, TOMORROW WE'LL BE SAILIN DOWN THE COAST OF THE KINGDOM OF JUDAEA. I PROMISE YOU'LL FINI THAT A MORE HOSPITABLE LAND!

NEXT MORNING...
THERE'S THE PROMISED LAND, ASTERIX!

GO TO JERUSALEM AND TELL SAMSON ALIUS I SENT YOU. HE'S MY SUPPLIER: YOU'LL BE ABLE TO GET ROCK OIL FROM HIM.

THANKS, EKONOMIKRISIS! SEE YOU SOON, MAYBE!
I HOPE SO! TRAVELLING WITH YOU IS AN ENRICHING EXPERIENCE!

AND I'M STILL HUNGRY! DO YOU THINK THERE ARE ANY WILD BOARS HERE?
NEVER MIND THAT. WE'VE GOT TO FIND OUR WAY!
25A

THERE'S SOMEONE WHO MIGHT BE ABLE TO HELP US!

HULLO, FRIEND! CAN YOU TELL US THE WAY TO JERUSALEM?
MY DONKEY AND I ARE GOING THERE OURSELVES! LET'S JOIN FORCES!

MY NAME'S JOSHUA BEN ZEDRIN.
I'M ASTERIX. MEET OBELIX, DOGMATIX, AND DUBBELOSIX THE DRUID!

WE'VE COME FROM GAUL TO BUY ROCK OIL FROM THE MERCHANT SAMSON ALIUS.
I WOULDN'T HAVE THOUGHT ANYONE WOULD COME SO FAR FOR THAT!

ARE THERE MANY ROMANS HERE?
NOT AS MANY AS IN PHOENICIA. THAT'S A ROMAN PROVINCE. WE'RE ONLY A PROTECTORATE, AND THE ROMANS DON'T HAVE A STRONG GARRISON IN JERUSALEM!
25B

* LEVITICUS 11, Vii

AT LAST, AFTER SEVERAL DAYS ON THE ROAD, OUR FRIENDS ARRIVE IN JERUSALEM, THE GREAT ROYAL CITY BEHIND ITS HIGH WALLS, LATER TO OPEN ITS GATES TO ALL THE FAITHS OF THE WORLD.

SHALOM, ISAIAH! WHAT'S NEW?
NOTHING MUCH, EXCEPT THAT THE ROMANS HAVE DOUBLED THEIR GUARD AND ARE KEEPING A CLOSE WATCH ON ALL THE CITY GATES.

WHAT ARE THEY LOOKING FOR?
THREE GAULS AND A DOG, AND IF I WERE YOUR FRIENDS I'D WATCH MY STEP!

GOOD, SO THE FLY GOT THROUGH AGAIN!
WE'LL SAY GOODBYE. WE DON'T WANT TO BRING YOU TROUBLE.
BUT WHY ARE THE ROMANS AFTER YOU?

THEY'RE TRYING TO STOP US BUYING SOME ROCK OIL TO TAKE BACK TO GAUL!
SO NOW THEY'RE PLANNING TO PUT SMALL TRADERS OUT OF BUSINESS!

FOLLOW ME! I'LL TAKE YOU TO A FRIEND OF MINE IN A VILLAGE NEAR JERUSALEM. THE ROMANS WILL NEVER THINK OF LOOKING FOR YOU THERE!
27A

AND TONIGHT WE'LL FIND SOME WAY TO GET YOU IN OVER THE WALLS!
WHY ARE YOU TAKING THE RISK OF HELPING US, JOSHUA?

ALL THE HEBREWS DISTRUST THE POWER OF ROME. WE MUST HELP THOSE WHO OPPOSE IT!

HERE WE ARE!

NEVER SAW SUCH AN PPETITE! THAT'S HIS ENTH STUFFED CARP, ND HE STILL WANTS MORE!
IF YOU'D LIKE A REST, I CAN ONLY OFFER YOU THE STABLE, BUT YOU'LL FIND IT'S QUITE COMFORTABLE!
I'LL COME AND FETCH YOU TONIGHT!

LATER, AT NIGHT...
HE WAS RIGHT, IT IS COMFORTABLE. WHAT'S THIS VILLAGE CALLED?
BETHLEHEM, I THINK.
27B

TIME TO LEAVE! THERE ARE FRIENDS WAITING FOR US ON THE WALLS OF JERUSALEM!

HERE WE ARE! KEEP QUIET: I'M AFRAID THE ROMANS MIGHT SURPRISE US!
THEY'RE THE ONES WHO'D BE SURPRISED!
I MUST TIP OFF THE SENTRIES SOMEHOW... SUPPOSE I TIP MYSELF OFF?

YOUR TURN!

HERE GOES!

OUCH!
?!

OUCH! EEK! OW!
I HURT MYSELF!
OH, SHUT HIM UP, OBELIX!!!

IF YOU'VE QUITE FINISHED WAILING..!
BONK!

THE... THE ROMANS!!!
GOODY, GOODY, GOODY!
IT'S THEM! GET THEM!
WOOF!

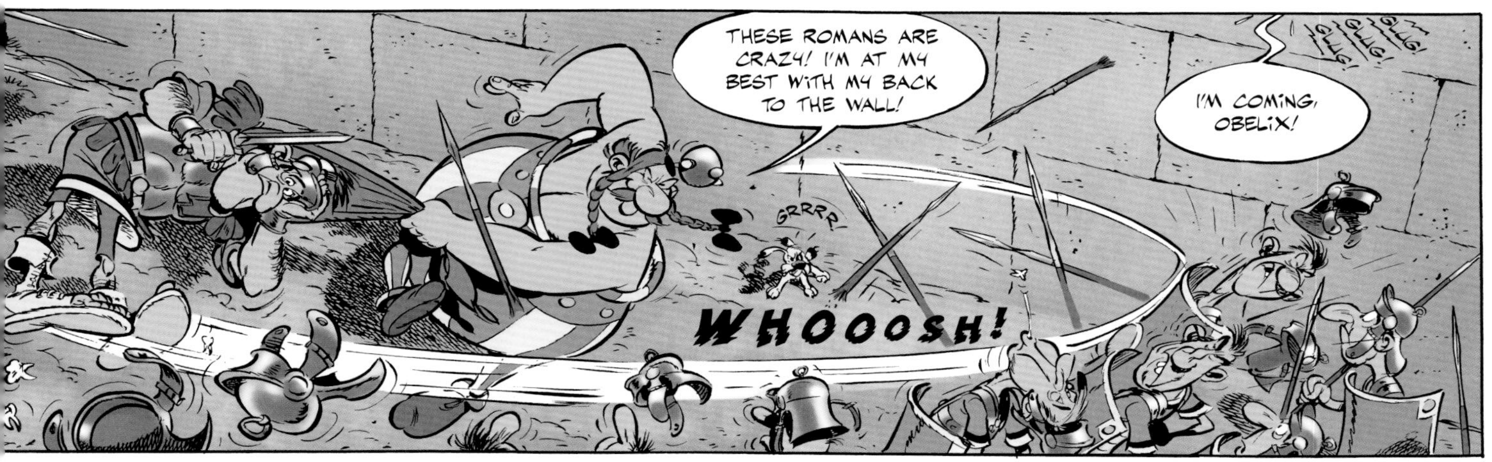
THESE ROMANS ARE CRAZY! I'M AT MY BEST WITH MY BACK TO THE WALL!
GRRRR
I'M COMING, OBELIX!
WHOOOSH!

BADABLAM!

QUICK, OVER THE WALL! THE ROMANS ARE ON THE ALERT NOW!
I WOULDN'T CALL THIS LOT VERY ALERT AT THE MOMENT.
YES, THEY SEEM A BIT SOFT ON TERRA FIRMA!
29 A

BY YAHVEH! YOU AND THOSE ROMANS... IT WAS LIKE DAVID FACING GOLIATH, BUT WHAT A BEATING THEY TOOK!
YES, AND I'M NOT SORRY TO BE RID OF THAT SPYING DRUID EITHER!

THIS IS WHERE SAMSON ALIAS THE MERCHANT LIVES.

CUSTOMERS FROM VERY FAR AWAY, SAMSON!
WE'D LIKE SOME ROCK OIL, AND WE'RE IN A GREAT HURRY!
OYOYOY! OH DEAR!

THE ROMANS HAVE JUST BURNT ALL OUR STOCKS, AND I VERY MUCH FEAR YOU WON'T FIND A SINGLE DROP IN THE WHOLE COUNTRY!
?!
29B

BUT WE MUST TAKE SOME ROCK OIL BACK TO GAUL! IT'S VITAL!
THEN YOU'LL HAVE TO LOOK WHERE THEY FIND IT: NEAR BABYLON IN MESOPOTAMIA!

HOW MANY MILES TO BABYLON?
WELL, IT'S THIRTY DAYS' JOURNEY, AND YOU'LL HAVE TO CROSS THE DESERT!

I'VE NEVER TRIED A DESERT CROSSING BEFORE, BUT BY TOUTATIS, I'M READY TO TACKLE IT!

HERE'S MY ASSISTANT, SAUL BEN EPHISHUL. AT SUNRISE HE WILL GUIDE YOU TO THE EDGE OF THE DESERT.
WEAR THESE AND YOU'LL PASS UNNOTICED.
HOW CAN WE THANK YOU?

OH, IF YOU'RE AIMING TO GIVE THE ROMANS TROUBLE, WE'RE QUITS!
BUT YOUR OWN NAME SOUNDS RATHER ROMAN, SAMSON ALIUS?

I TOOK THIS ALIAS FOR BUSINESS REASONS. MY REAL NAME IS ROSEN-BLUMENTHALOVITCH!

AND AT DAWN...
GOOD LUCK!
MAZEL TOV!
YOU'RE RIGHT, WE DO PASS UNNOTICED IN THIS DISGUISE!
AND THE STRIPES ARE VERY SLIMMING, TOO!
WOOF!
WOOF!

THE ROMAN
OCURATOR'S PALACE...
AVE, O PONTIUS PIRATE! THE GAULS GOT AWAY, AND WE FEAR THEY'VE MADE GOOD THEIR ESCAPE NOW!
ONCE THEY'RE OUTSIDE MY TERRITORY, MY DEAR DUBBELOSIX, I COULDN'T CARE LESS WHAT THEY DO!
I WISH HE'D STOP WASHING HIS HANDS THE WHOLE TIME!

WELL, NEVER MIND! ASTERIX AND OBELIX ARE BOUND TO GO BACK ON BOARD SHIP, AND WHEN THEY DO WE'LL BE WAITING, WITH QUITE A RECEPTION COMMITTEE!

NWHILE...
WE'RE COMING TO THE DEAD SEA!
IT MAKES ME SICK, ASTERIX!
I HAVE TO ADMIT THESE MOUNTS ARE RATHER BUMPY!

I DIDN'T MEAN THAT! IT MAKES ME SICK TO THINK OF THE RACIAL DISCRIMINATION PRACTISED AGAINST BOARS IN THIS COUNTRY!
?!?
31 A

THE SEA!
YIPPEE!!!

IT'S SO HOT I COULD DO WITH A NICE DIP!
HEY, WAIT!

HERE GOES!

?
FLOP!
FLOP!
FLOP!
FLOP!

I WAS GOING TO WARN YOU: THE DEAD SEA HAS A SALT CONTENT SIX TIMES HIGHER THAN THAT OF OTHER SEAS, AND ITS DENSITY IS SUCH THAT THE HUMAN BODY JUST FLOATS ON TOP!
HOHOHO! HAHA!
ARF! ARF! ARF!
31 B

WE'RE ON THE OUTSKIRTS OF THE DESERT WHERE I MUST LEAVE YOU. YOU'LL FIND YOUR WAY TO MESO-POTAMIA QUITE EASILY: JUST GO STRAIGHT EAST!
THANKS AGAIN, SAUL BEN EPHISHUL!

THE DESERT IS BURNING HOT BY DAY...

...AND FREEZING COLD BY NIGHT.
THIS DESERT IS CRAZY!

THIRTY DAYS OF THIS IS GOING TO BE MONOTONOUS!

?!
PLUNK!

QUICK, LET'S TAKE COVER!

WHO ARE YOU?
WE ARE ARMORICAN GAULS!

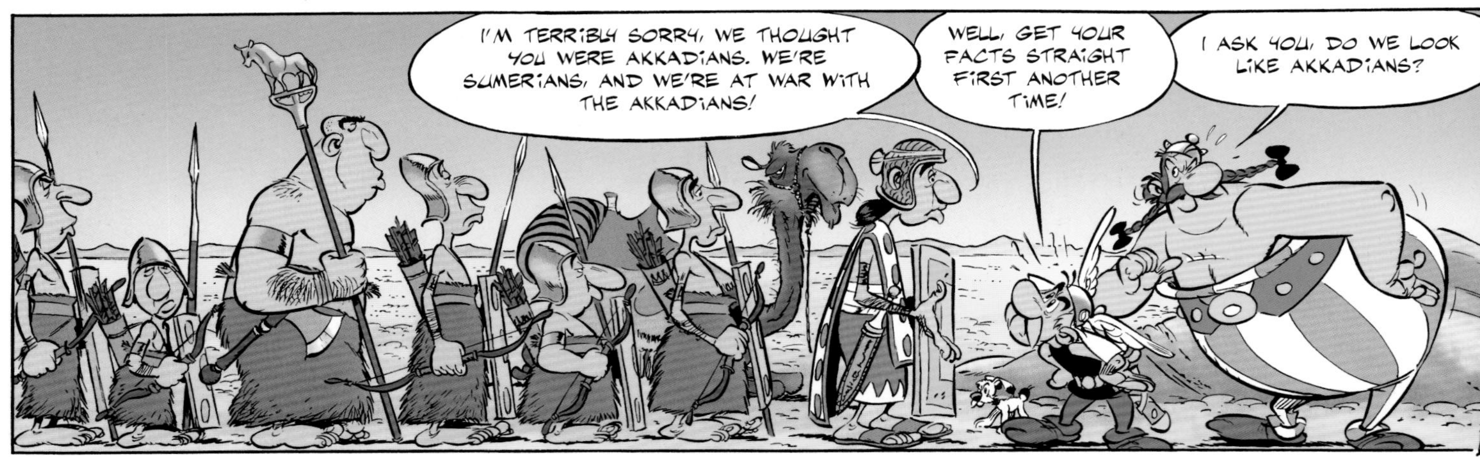
I'M TERRIBLY SORRY, WE THOUGHT YOU WERE AKKADIANS. WE'RE SUMERIANS, AND WE'RE AT WAR WITH THE AKKADIANS!
WELL, GET YOUR FACTS STRAIGHT FIRST ANOTHER TIME!
I ASK YOU, DO WE LOOK LIKE AKKADIANS?

PHEW! THE HEAT WAS REALLY ON!
THESE SUMERIANS ARE CRAZY!
TAP! TAP! TAP!

!
PLUNK!

TAKE COVER!

WHO ARE YOU?
WE ARE GAULS!

OH, TERRIBLY SORRY. WE THOUGHT YOU WERE HITTITES! WE AKKADIANS DON'T HIT IT OFF WITH THE HITTITES. WE'RE AT WAR WITH THEM!
WELL, DON'T DRAG US IN!
I ASK YOU, DO WE LOOK LIKE HITTITES?
33A

D I THOUGHT HINGS WERE OING TO BE ONOTONOUS!
THESE AKKADIANS ARE CRAZY!
TAP! TAP! TAP!

!
PLUNK!

... COVER!!!

WHO ARE YOU?
WE'RE GAULS!

WE'RE SO SORRY, WE THOUGHT YOU WERE ASSYRIANS! WE HITTITES ARE AT WAR WITH THE ASSYRIANS!
I ASK YOU, DO WE LOOK LIKE ASSYRIANS?
33B

THESE HITTITES ARE CRAZY!
THIS IS CERTAINLY A CROWDED PART OF THE DESERT!
TAP! TAP!

PLUNK!

WHO ARE...
GAULS!

I KNOW, YOU'RE A COHORT OF ASSYRIANS COMING DOWN LIKE A WOLF ON THE FOLD AND YOU'RE TERRIBLY SORRY! JUST WHO DID YOU THINK WE WERE?
ER... WELL, MEDES!

I ASK YOU, DO WE LOOK LIKE MEDES? THESE ASSYRIANS ARE...
TAP! TAP!

!
EXCUSE ME, GENTLEMEN. WE ARE MEDES, LOST IN THIS DESERT!

COULD YOU POSSIBLY TELL US THE WAY OUT?

NOTHING EASIER! JUST FOLLOW THE ARROWS!
?!

YOU KNOW, THESE MEDES ARE...
TAP! TAP!

STOP IT!! YOU'RE GETTING ME DOWN, SAYING THE SAME THING OVER AND OVER AGAIN!

WELL! THIS GAUL IS CRAZY!
TAP! TAP! TAP!

I'M THIRSTY ASTERIX!
HAVE A DRINK OF WATER!

I CAN'T. IT'S RUN OUT.
?!?

AN ARROW PIERCED THE WATER SKIN!
!!
35A

WE'LL NEVER REACH BYLON WITHOUT WATER! AT MEANS NO ROCK OIL AND NO MORE MAGIC OTION! WE'VE FAILED, LESS WE FIND HELP. OH, ONLY WE COULD MEET SOMEONE!
JUST NOW YOU WERE COMPLAINING THE PLACE WAS CROWDED...

OBELIX, YOU REALLY DO GET ME DOWN!!!
LOOK AT DOGMATIX!

LOOKS AS IF HE'S FOUND SOMETHING!
SNIFF! SNIFF!

YBE HE'S SCOVERED SPRING!
WHY NOT? DOGMATIX CAN FIND ANYTHING! YOU ONLY HAVE TO ASK HIM!
SCRATCH! SCRATCH!

WHOOOOOOOOOOOO
?!?
SCRATCH! SCRATCH!

OOOOOOOOOO
?
SCRATCH! SCRATCH! SCRATCH!
35B

!?!
BRAOM

YUK! THIS WATER TASTES HORRIBLE AND IT'S ALL BLACK!

WE'VE STRUCK ROCK OIL!
IT'S LIQUID GOLD! IT'S THE BLACK GOLD WE NEED!

FANTASTIC! NOW WE NEEDN'T GO TO BABYLON!
DIDN'T I TELL YOU DOGMATIX COULD FIND ANYTHING?

I'VE REPAIRED THE WATER SKIN. LET'S FILL IT WITH OIL AND GET OUT OF THIS DESERT FAST!

LATER...
NOW TO REJOIN EKONOMIKRISIS AND HIS SHIP AT TYRE AND GET BACK TO GAUL AT TOP SPEED!

?
WOOF! WOOF!
I CAN SMELL THE ROAST BOAR ALREADY!

BUT IN PREFECT CLASSIS TYRANNICUS'S PALACE IN TYRE...
WHO ARE YOU AND WHAT DO YOU WANT, STRANGER?
I AM SENT BY CAESAR, WHO HAS JUST GOT THIS MESSAGE THROUGH TO ME. YOU ARE TO GIVE ORDERS TO HAVE ALL MERCHANT VESSELS ABOUT TO SET SAIL FOR GAUL DESTROYED AND SUNK!
BZZZ

TALK ABOUT WINGED WORDS! YOUR MESSENGER DID WELL TO DO THE JOURNEY FROM ROME TO TYRE SO FAST!
YES, A REALLY TOP FLIGHT MESSENGER!
BZZZZZZ!

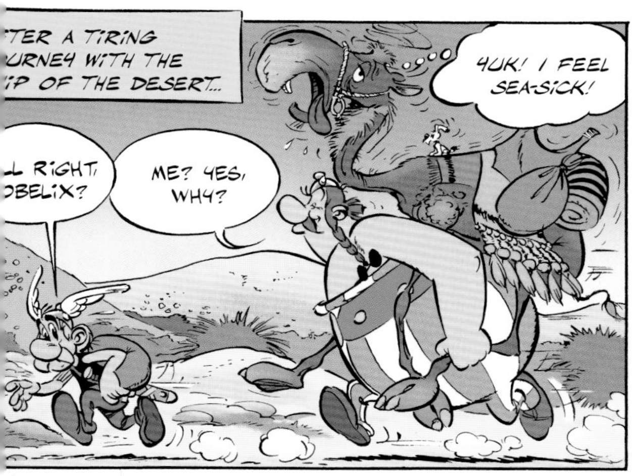
TER A TIRING
URNEY WITH THE
IP OF THE DESERT...
YUK! I FEEL SEA-SICK!
L RIGHT, OBELIX?
ME? YES, WHY?

...OUR FRIENDS RETURN TO TYRE.
LET'S USE SAMSON ALIUS'S DISGUISES AGAIN, TO HELP US GET INTO THE PORT UNNOTICED!
BEING HUMPED ABOUT REALLY GIVES ME THE HUMP!

THE PLACE IS FULL OF ROMANS. WE MUST BE CAREFUL!

HOW SHALL WE EVER FIND EKONOMIKRISIS IN ALL THIS?
I'VE GOT AN IDEA!
37A

'SCUSE ME, SOLDIER...
MPH?

WHERE CAN WE FIND EKONOMIKRISIS, PLEASE?
THE PHOENICIAN MERCHANT? HIS WAREHOUSE IS AT THE END OF THE PORT JUST GO STRAIGHT AHEAD YOU CAN'T MISS IT AND NOW WOULD YOU KINDLY PUT ME DOWN?

BLING!

YOU SEE? GOOD
NNERS WILL GET YOU ANYWHERE!
OH, WHAT A BRILLIANTLY STRIKING IDEA! YOU'LL BRING THE WHOLE ROMAN GARRISON OF TYRE DOWN ON US!

EKONOMIKRISIS
IMPORT - EXPORT
OF COURSE, WHEN IT'S NOT MISTER ASTERIX'S IDEA...
HERE WE ARE!
THERE THEY ARE. AFTER THEM!
37B

QUICK, EKONOMIKRISIS, WE MUST WEIGH ANCHOR! WHERE'S YOUR SHIP?
GONE! I HAVEN'T GOT A SHIP NOW!

WHAT DO YOU MEAN, GONE?
THE ROMANS SANK MY SHIP ON JULIUS CAESAR'S ORDERS. YOU FIND ME SUNK IN GLOOM: MY BIGGEST ASSET'S BEEN LIQUIDATED!

I MIGHT HAVE KNOWN DUBBELOSIX WOULD WARN THE ROMANS TO STOP US SETTING SAIL FOR GAUL AGAIN!

THEY'RE IN HERE!!! SEARCH THIS WAREHOUSE!
HERE! FOLLOW ME!

WHEN THE ROMANS STARTED TAXING ME I BUILT THIS TUNNEL. IT LEADS TO A CELLAR...

...WHERE I HIDE MOST OF MY STOCK. THAT WAY I'M ALWAYS IN A SELLER'S MARKET!

WE'RE JUST BELOW THE MAIN QUAY...

...AND IRONICALLY, OPPOSITE JULIUS CAESAR'S FLAGSHIP!

YOU MEAN CAESAR'S HERE?
NO, BUT HE'S LENT THE SHIP TO THE HEAD OF M.I.VI, WHO'S HERE TO SEE YOU CAPTURED!

SURE ENOUGH, ON BOARD CAESAR'S GALLEY...
CAESAR IS GETTING IMPATIENT, DUBBELOSIX! WHAT ABOUT THAT MAGIC POTION?
I ONLY HAVE TO DISPOSE OF ASTERIX AND OBELIX, WHICH SHOULDN'T TAKE LONG. THEY'VE JUST BEEN SPOTTED IN HEBREW DISGUISE!
BZZZ

I'VE GOT AN IDEA!
HUH! COPYCAT!

IS YOUR CREW STILL AROUND, EKONOMIKRISIS?
YES, BUT THEY'RE NOT PACKAGE TOURISTS NOW. THEY'RE THE WINNERS OF A COMPETITION... ALL THE PRIZES WERE A SEA CRUISE EXCLUSIVE OF EXPENSES. I'M THEIR C.O.: COMPETITION ORGANISER.

THEN GET THEM HERE! NOW, THIS IS WHAT WE'LL DO...
39A

AT NIGHT-FALL...

EVENING, SOLDIER!
HALT!!! WHO GOES THERE?

YOU'RE IN LUCK, GAUL: FOR A MOMENT I THOUGHT YOU WERE IN HEBREW DISGUI...

BING!

QUICK! LET'S GET THE CARGO ON BOARD!
39B

WELL, IF IT ISN'T AN OLD FRIEND OF MINE!
ASTERIX!
THE GAUL?

POC!

LEAVE IT TO ME! I'LL TAKE THE SHIP OUT OF HARBOUR!

THEY REALLY ARE GOOD SAILSMEN AS WELL AS GOO SALESMEN! THEY SHOULD B PHOENICIAN!

JULIUS CAESAR WILL NOT BE PLEASED!
OH YES, HE WILL! JULIUS CAESAR WILL BE DELIGHTED TO GET THE MESSAGE I'M SENDING HIM!

OFF YOU GO, MY PRETTY, TAKING WITH YOU THE VENGEANCE OF DUBBELOSIX!!!
HIS HONEYED VOICE CAN ALWAYS WIN ME OVER!

LATER, IN ROME...
A MESSAGE FOR YOU, O CAESAR! NOT IN VERY GOOD CONDITION: THE BEARER FELL INTO MY SOUP!
GIVE IT HERE!

'THE INDOMITABLE GAULS HAVE NO MAGIC POTION LEFT, AND CANNOT MAKE ANY MORE. NOW THERE IS NOTHING TO PREVENT YOUR LEGIONS OCCUPYING ALL GAUL. DUBBELOSIX.'

QUICK! GIVE ORDERS TO INVADE AND CRUSH THE GAULISH VILLAGE!

E RETURN JOURNEY IS
PLEASANT IF ROUTINE
D OF CRUISE...
PIRATE SHIP AHOY, C.O.!
CUSTOMERS!

ROMAN GALLEY TO STARBOARD!
WE'RE NEUTRAL! EVERYONE KNOWS THAT! I WAIVE THIS ONE... LET THE ROMANS RULE THE WAVES!

BUT THEY'RE NOT WAVERING! THEY'RE GIVING CHASE!
?!

TER...
FOUR THOUSAND ESTERTII! THAT'S IT!
BUT THAT'S TWICE LAST TIME'S PRICE!
YOU KNOW HOW IT IS WITH THE INFLATION!

HOW WOULD YOU LIKE TO GO INTO BUSINESS WITH ME?
AVE ATQUE VALE!
NEVER MIND THE VEILED REFERENCES, HOW AM I GOING TO SELL THIS LOT?
FLOAT A COMPANY!
41A

WELL, WE ARE BRINGING ROCK OIL BACK TO GAUL IN SPITE OF YOU, DUBBELOSIX!

?!
I'M NOT SO SURE ABOUT THAT!

NO, OBELIX! NOOOO!

PRRRFFFFF
BONG!
WOOF! WOOF!

AND THE WATERS OF THE CHANNEL ARE POLLUTED FOR THE FIRST TIME IN HISTORY.
OH NO! DON'T SAY YOU'RE STARTING ALREADY?!
41B

WE'RE DONE FOR!
SLAP! SLAP! SLAP! SLAP! SLAP! SLAP!

WE'VE SIGHTED ARMORICA, C.O.!
DONE FOR!

GOODBYE! I PROMISE TO BRING YOU BACK SOME ROCK OIL ON MY NEXT VOYAGE, ASTERIX!
DONE FOR!

THE WHOLE VILLAGE WILL BE WAITING ON TENTERHOOK AND IN FEAR OF THE ROMAN AND NOW WHAT AM I GOING TO TELL THEM?

?
THEY'RE RUNNING LIKE RABBITS!
WHAT A SHAME! WE WERE HAVING FUN!
AT WHAT AGE CAN A LEGIONA RETIRE IN GOO ORDER?

BUT... BUT THEY'RE FIGHTING!
WITHOUT POTION!!
WITHOUT US EITHER. IT'S NOT FAIR!

GETAFIX, WHAT IS THIS MIRACLE? WHAT'S GOING ON?
HULLO, ASTERIX, HAD A NICE TRIP?

I'M AFRAID I HAVEN'T BROUGHT ANY ROCK OIL BACK, GETAFIX!
ANY WHAT OIL?

ROCK OIL, OF COURSE! BLACK GOLD! THE VITAL GREDIENT OF THE MAGIC POTION!
OH, YES, PETRA OLEUM!

DON'T WORRY! FORTUNATELY, AFTER CONDUCTING A FEW EXPERIMENTS, I MANAGED TO SUBSTITUTE BEETROOT JUICE INSTEAD. WE RUN JUST AS WELL ON BEETROOT JUICE, AND IT TASTES NICER!
BONK!

?
43A

S A STROKE! E SEEN THIS EFORE. MY OTHER-IN-LAW HAD ONE WHEN...
WANT ME TO THUMP YOU?
GO AWAY! I'LL TREAT HIM FOR SHOCK.

YOU'RE RIGHT. THE NEW MAGIC POTION DOES TASTE NICER, BUT ANOTHER TIME I WISH YOU'D CONDUCT YOUR EXPERIMENTS BEFORE SENDING US TO THE ENDS OF THE EARTH, GETAFIX!
I WILL, ASTERIX.

HEY, ASTERIX, WHAT SHALL WE DO WITH THESE TWO?
WHAT WITH ALL THE EXCITEMENT I'D ALMOST FORGOTTEN THEM!

IS DUBBELOSIX'S CHARIOT STILL AROUND?
DON'T MENTION THAT CHARIOT TO ME! I TRIED USING IT, AND IT TURNED INTO A TRUNK! I WAS SHUT INSIDE IT FOR THREE DAYS BEFORE ANYONE COULD GET ME OUT!

EXACTLY WHAT I NEED!
43B

LATER, IN ROME...
AVE, CAESAR! THIS GIFT-WRAPPED TRUNK HAS JUST COME FOR YOU!
OPEN IT!

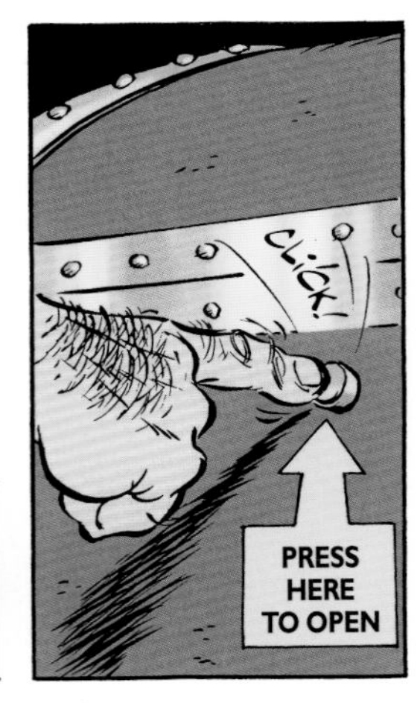
CLICK!
PRESS HERE TO OPEN

CLING!
CLANG!
THE GAULISH VILLAGE with Compliments to Caesar

WHAT'S THE IDEA OF THE BRUSH AND THE JAR OF HONEY?
Honey

THEY'RE PART OF A NEW GAME CAESAR'S INVENTED FOR THE CIRCUS!
BZZZZZZZZ
BZZZZZZ

UNDER A CLOUDLESS SKY, FAR FROM SUCH CRUEL AND BARBAROUS PASTIMES, THE INDOMITABLE GAULS OF THE VILLAGE GIVE THEMSELVES UP TO HEALTHIER PLEASURES. THEY HAVE NO PETRA OLEUM, BUT THEY ARE NOT SHORT OF IDEAS FOR CELEBRATING THE RETURN OF THE HEROES.
HAVE YOU EVER THOUGHT OF COOKING STUFFED BOAR?
?
COME ON, ASTERIX, TELL US ABOUT YOUR ADVENTURES!
WELL, IT ALL BEGAN IN THE QUIET, PEACEFUL DEPTHS OF THE GAULISH FOREST, WHERE EVERYTHING SEEMED TO INDICATE THAT IT WAS DINNER TIME...
SCRONTCH!
THE HOLIDAYS ARE OVER!
UDERZO 8-81
THE END

R. GOSCINNY ASTERIX A. UDERZO

ASTERIX and Son

Written and illustrated by Albert UDERZO

GOSCINNY AND UDERZO

PRESENT

An Asterix Adventure

ASTERIX AND SON

Written and Illustrated by ALBERT UDERZO

Translated by Anthea Bell *and* Derek Hockridge

Orion
Children's Books

E SUN IS RISING OVER ASTERIX'S VILLAGE, AS USUAL.
E SCENE IS ONE OF PEACE AND SERENITY...

...DISTURBED, DESPITE THE FACT THAT DAY IS DAWNING, BY THE SNORES OF THE ONLY GAULISH ROOSTER WHO HAS ADENOIDS.
SNORT!
ZZZ!

IT'S COCKCROW, YOU GOOSE! TIME TO TALK TURKEY.
TAP! TAP! TAP!
YOU'RE IN A FOWL MOOD THIS MORNING!

COCK-A-DOODLE-DOO
YAWN!
COME ON, GET UP! IT'S GOING TO BE A LOVELY DAY!

I HAD SUCH A FUNNY DREAM LAST NIGHT, ASTERIX!
SCRATCH! SCRATCH!
1A

I DREAMED THE STORKS VISITED OUR VILLAGE, BRINGING THE BABIES EOPLE HAD ORDERED, AND NE OF THEM LEFT A BABY HERE BY MISTAKE!
SCRATCH! SCRATCH!

DON'T SAY YOU STILL BELIEVE STORKS DELIVER BABIES!
WHY NOT? I DELIVER MENHIRS, DON'T I?

ONE OF THESE DAYS YOU AND I MUST HAVE A LITTLE TALK, OBELIX!

CREEAK!
GA! GA!

?
GOO! GOO!

GURGLE!
1B

IT... IT CAN'T BE TRUE! THIS MUST BE SOME KIND OF JOKE!

WAAAAAAAH!
OBELIX!
SCRAPE! SCRAPE!
?

WHAT IS IT?
GUESS!!!
WAAAH!

THERE! STORKS DO DELIVER BABIES, AND THEY MADE A MISTAKE!
WAAAH!
OBELIX, YOU'RE GETT ME DOWN! H ME CALM T BABY DOW INSTEAD!
?

WAAAH!
MAYBE HE'S HUNGRY?
OH DEAR... I FINISHED UP THE LAST BOAR YESTERDAY EVENING!

AAH!
I'VE AN IDEA BABIES DRINK MILK!
OH, I KNOW WHERE TO GET MILK!

WAAAH!
WHAT'S ALL THAT YELLING?
IS CACOFONIX THE BARD PRACTISING?

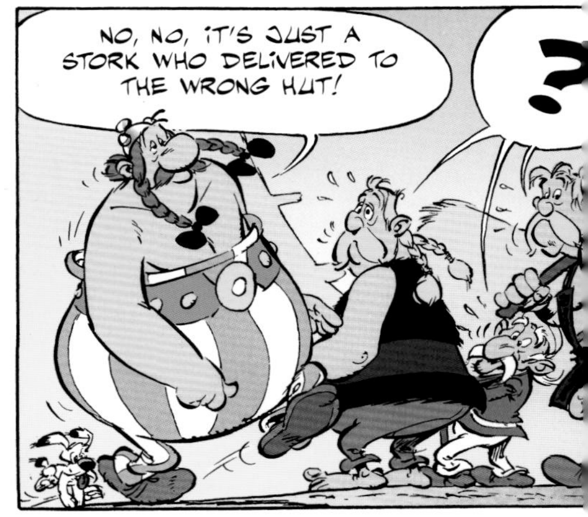
NO, NO, IT'S JUST A STORK WHO DELIVERED TO THE WRONG HUT!
?

MOOOOOOO!
DING!
DING!
I BORROWED BUCOLIX'S COW IN EXCHANGE FOR A MENHIR, ASTERIX!
?
WAAAH!

WAAAAH!
WELL, NEVER MIND ALL THAT NOW! MILK THE COW AND LET'S GET IT OVER WITH!

MOOOOOOO!
PSSS! PSSS! COME ON, HURRY UP! PSSS! PSSS!
WAAAH!
!

YES, WELL, I CAN SEE YOU KNOW AS MUCH ABOUT COWS AS STORKS! HOLD THIS BABY AND I'LL DO IT!
WAAAH!
3A

HE... HE'S WET THROUGH!
AND WHOSE FAULT IS THAT?
WAAAH!

SOON AFTER...
WAAAH!
I'VE MILKED THE COW. NOW FIND SOMETHING TO USE AS A BOTTLE WHILE I CHANGE HIM!

LOOK, I SWOPPED A SHOP-SOILED MENHIR FOR A GOURD WITH A TEAT!
GOO!
TEAT FOR TAT, EH?

HUH!
YOU FEED HIM WHILE I SUMMON THE VILLAGE COUNCIL!

BUT I DON'T KNOW HOW A BABY FEEDS!
NEVER MIND. HE DOES!
GA! GA!

I FEEL AS IF THE WHOLE WORLD WAS WATCHING ME AND LAUGHING!
GLUG!
GLUG!
GLUG!
HARF!
HARF!
HARF!
3B

I SEE YOUR PROBLEM, ASTERIX! WE MUST FIND OUT WHERE THE BABY COMES FROM AND WHOSE HE IS. IT'S URGENT!

I MUST JUST POINT OUT THAT FOUNDLINGS ARE USUALLY DUMPED ON TEMPLE DOORSTEPS OR IN PUBLIC PLACES...

...SO THAT WHEN A BABY IS RATHER POINTEDLY LEFT OUTSIDE A BACHELOR WARRIOR'S HUT, PEOPLE ARE BOUND TO THINK THINGS!
THINGS? WHAT THINGS?

HEY! HANG ON! ARE YOU OUT OF YOUR MINDS?
TAP! TAP! TAP!

ONE MIGHT EVEN THINK MISTER ASTERIX WOULD HAVE NO TROUBLE IN FINDING THAT BABY'S MOTHER!
YOU DON'T MINCE YOUR WORDS, DO YOU? SHUT UP, OR I'LL MAKE MINCEMEAT OF YOU!
CALM DOWN! WE MUSTN'T GET UPSET!

Asterix! COME QUICK!!!
THAT'S OBELIX CALLING ME!!!

ASTERIiiiiiiX!
AND IT LOOKED LIKE BEING SUCH A LOVELY DAY!
MOOOOOOOO!
DING! DING! DING!

DING DING
DING
HE TAKES BUCOLIX'S COW FOR A RATTLE, ASTERIX!
MOOOOOOOO!
?
DING
DING DING!
GOO, GOO!

BY TOUTATIS, I BET YOU WENT AND MADE HIS BOTTLE OUT OF A GOURD WHICH WAS STILL HALF FULL OF MAGIC POTION!

WON'T IT BAD FOR GETAFIX?
DON'T WORRY! OBELIX IS LIVING PROOF OF THE FACT MAGIC POTION IS HARMLESS TO BABIES...

GA!
SPLATCH!
THOUGH MAYBE NOT TO THOSE IN THEIR VICINITY!
GEDOING!

GOTTA LOTTA BOTTLE, EH? YOU WANT A SMACKED BOTTOM!
GA?

GNNNNNNNN!

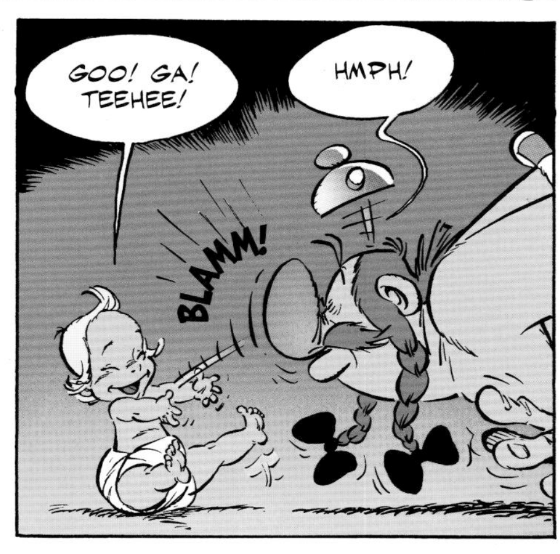
GOO! GA! TEEHEE!
HMPH!
BLAMM!

DON'T KNOW HAT BABIES E COMING TO HESE DAYS, ASTERIX!

HERE'S YOUR COW... A BIT RATTLED, BUT OK!
?!

AND NEXT TIME SHE SEES A BABY, MIND SHE DOESN'T LOOK SO LIKE A TOY! RATTLING COWS IS BAD FOR THEM!
??? ??? ?

CHIEF VITALSTATISTIX, WHAT AM I GOING TO DO ABOUT THIS BABY?
CLUCK!

DON'T YOU THINK YOU'VE DONE ENOUGH ALREADY?

AND DON'T TOUCH THAT CHILD WITH YOUR CLUMSY GREAT HANDS! WHAT HE NEEDS IS A MOTHER'S TENDER CARE!

DON'T YOU, MY LITTLE SWEETIE-PIE?
GA?

POC!

?

YOU COME HOME WITH ME! AND IN FUTURE, I DON'T WANT YOU MIXING WITH PEOPLE WHOSE EFFECT ON ALL AROUND THEM IS SO DEVASTATING!
BUT IMPEDIMENTA, DEAR...
?
CLUCK!

I THINK THIS BABY HAS HIS HEAD SCREWED ON THE RIGHT WAY!
GA!

HE'S DEFINITELY PICKED YOU TWO FOR HIS ADOPTIVE FATHERS!

ASTERIX AND OBELIX, THE GUARDIANSHIP OF THIS CHILD, WITH ALL ITS WEIGHTY RESPONSIBILITIES, IS NOW YOURS. TAKE GOOD CARE OF HIM!
I WILL NOW GIVE YOU AN ODE ON THE JOYS OF FAMILY LIFE!

'S GONE TO SLEEP! BIGGER THAN A WILD AR PIGLET, AND HE'S MUCH TROUBLE MAKING FTY MENHIRS!
WHO ON EARTH CAN HAVE BEEN BOLD ENOUGH TO ABANDON THIS BABY?

I TOLD YOU. IT MUST HAVE BEEN A STORK WHO...
SHUT UP ABOUT STORKS, OR I SHALL DO YOU AN INJURY!

SSSH! YOU'LL WAKE HIM UP, AND THEN HE'LL WANT A COW TO RATTLE!
THAT'S WHAT COMES OF BEING FOOL ENOUGH TO GIVE HIM A BOTTLE OF MILK WITH MAGIC POTION IN IT!

RK AT MISTER ASTERIX! LL OF THE MILK OF HUMAN DNESS, AREN'T YOU? WHO'S A MILKSOP, THEN?

MILKSOP YOURSELF! IT'S YOUR SOPPY FAULT!

OH, REALLY? YOU DON'T BELIEVE IN BOTTLING UP A GRIEVANCE DO YOU?
YOU'RE ENOUGH TO MAKE ME TAKE TO THE BOTTLE MYSELF!

WAAAAA!
!

AAAA!
THERE! WHAT DID I TELL YOU?
I THINK IT'S HIGH TIME WE WENT IN SEARCH OF THAT BABY'S PARENTS!

SO A LITTLE LATER...
ASTERIX, HOW ARE WE GOING TO RECOGNIZE PARENTS WHO WON'T EVEN RECOGNIZE THEIR OWN CHILD?
WE DO HAVE ONE CLUE: THE BABY'S CLOTHES AND WRAPPINGS ARE MADE OF EMBROIDERED LINEN, THE SORT OF THING YOU'D EXPECT TO FIND IN A RICH ROMAN FAMILY...

WE'LL START INVESTIGATING E FORTIFIED AN CAMPS THAT URROUND THE VILLAGE!
OH, GOODY! I LOVE INVESTIGATING ROMAN CAMPS!

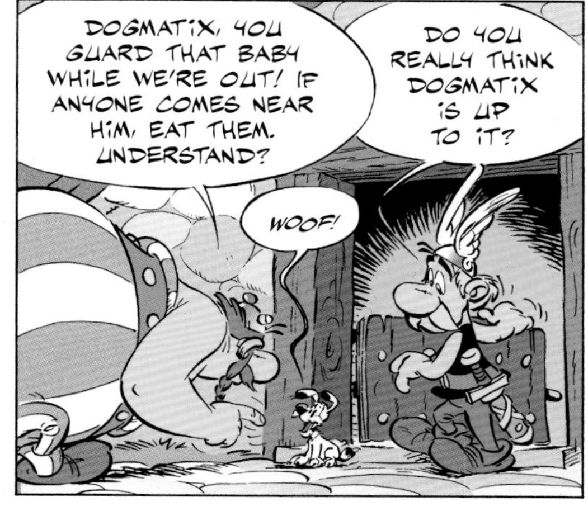
DOGMATIX, YOU GUARD THAT BABY WHILE WE'RE OUT! IF ANYONE COMES NEAR HIM, EAT THEM. UNDERSTAND?
DO YOU REALLY THINK DOGMATIX IS UP TO IT?
WOOF!

OF COURSE! HE'S HAD LOTS OF EXPERIENCE. I'VE TAUGHT HIM TO GUARD MENHIRS!
!!!

* FORWARD! MARCH! CHARGE! TO ARMS! TAKE AIM!

* RENN

SOME NEW ROMAN REINFORCEMENTS AT LAST! WHAT FUN!

?
?
WOOF!
WOOF!
WOOF!
WOOF!

THAT'S OGMATIX ARKING!
I HOPE THE BABY'S ALL RIGHT!
WOOF!
WOOF!
WOOF!
WOOF!

?!
GRRRRR
WOOF!
GA!

OW DID HE CATCH UP WITH US SO FAST?
HE'S STILL WELL TANKED UP WITH MAGIC POTION!

NOW WHAT DO WE DO, ASTERIX?
OH, TAKE HIM WITH US... IT'LL SIMPLIFY OUR INVESTIGATIONS!

TEEHEE! GOO!
SEE HOW HE MADE STRAIGHT FOR ME WHEN HE FELT LONELY?
YES, I EXPECT HE WANTED TO CHEW THE FAT?

'S NOT CHEWING E, AND ANYWAY, WHAT DO YOU MEAN, FAT!

THERE'S COMPENDIUM! THIS INVESTIGATION CALLS FOR TACT AND DELICACY... YOU KNOW WHAT TO DO, OBELIX?
YES. WE SMASH OUR WAY IN, ASK PEOPLE TO PUT THEIR HEADS TOGETHER, AND DO IT FOR THEM IF THEY WON'T!

RAISE THE ALARM!

CLOCK!

I DO LIKE YOUR TACT AND DELICACY, ASTERIX!

I TRY NOT TO BE A CRASHING BORE MYSELF WHEN I PAY CALLS!
CRASH!
HA, HA! GA!

HERE, WHAT'S THE IDEA?
WE'RE INVESTIGATING! ONLY PASSING THROUGH!
PAF!
PIF!
WELL, THERE'S NO CALL TO MAKE US PASS OUT!

DO YOU RECOGNIZE THIS BABY?
I'VE RECOGNIZED FOURTEEN BABIES WAITING FOR ME BACK IN ROME, BUT I'M ALMOST CERTAIN THAT'S NOT ONE OF MINE!

LET'S TRY THE CAMP OF LAUDANUM...

BUT IN THE CAMPS OF LAUDANUM...

...AND TOTORUM, THE INVESTIGATIONS GET NOWHERE.
SO THAT'S WHAT THEY CALL AN OPINION POLL?

ELL, NOW FOR QUARIUM, THE AST FORTIFIED ROMAN CAMP!

SOON AFTERWARDS...
WE'RE TRYING TO FIND OUT WHO ABANDONED THIS BABY AND MAKING SOME INVESTIGATIONS!
YOUR METHODS ARE CERTAINLY STRIKING!

I KNOW SOMEONE WHO MAY BE ABLE TO HELP YOU!

WE HAD A VISIT FROM A PREFECT THIS MORNING. HE'S GOING AROUND TAKING A CENSUS OF ALL THE LOCAL GAULS!
WE KNOW THAT! SO?

SO THAT'S JUST A PRETEXT! THE PREFECT TOLD ME HIS REAL JOB WAS TO LOOK FOR A BABY. IT MIGHT WELL BE THIS ONE!
11A

QUICK, OBELIX! E MUST FIND THAT PREFECT AGAIN!
ROMAN CAMPS ARE LIKE POCKETS... YOU NEVER FIND WHAT YOU'RE AFTER TILL YOU GET TO THE LAST ONE!

IF SO MANY RESOURCES ARE BEING DEPLOYED TO FIND HIM, THAT BABY MUST BELONG TO A POWERFUL FAMILY!
THAT'S WHAT MAKES HIM SO STRONG! NOTHING TO DO WITH THE POTION, EH, MY BOY?
GA!

CAREFUL! HEAR VOICES!!!

AND THE PREFECT SAID NOT TO WORRY, TAKING A CENSUS IS DEAD EASY, HE SAID! EASY AND SAFE... ALL YOU HAVE TO KNOW IS HOW TO COUNT, HE SAID!
YEAH... COUNT YOUR BRUISES!
WELL HE CAN'T COUNT ON ME ANY MORE!
QUOD ERAT DEMONSTRANDUM!
SHUT UP AND KEEP LIMPING!
11B

THE GAULS!
CALM DOWN, ROMANS! JUST TAKE US TO YOUR LEADER, PREFECT CACTUS! WE WANT TO TALK TO HIM!
STAY HERE AND BE GOOD, OKAY?
GA?
GRRRR!

HE CAST US ASIDE LIKE AN OLD DIGITABULUM* AND HE WENT OFF TO CONDATUM IN A HURRY!

* ROMAN GLOVE

OHO! THIS MUST BE THE BABY CRISMUS CACTUS IS, LIKE, Y'KNOW, LOOKING FOR! IF I TAKE HIM THE CHILD HE'LL MAKE ME SORT OF OPTIO, Y'KNOW, AND COVER ME, LIKE, WITH GOLD!

SO WHO'S COUNTING ON THE RESULTS OF THIS CENSUS?

NOT CAESAR, ANYWAY. HE'S BUSY WITH THE TROUBLES IN UPPER GERMANIA!
I'LL SEIZE MY CHANCE WHILE THEY'RE ALL, LIKE, TALKING! TEEHEE!

HELP! HELP
?
?

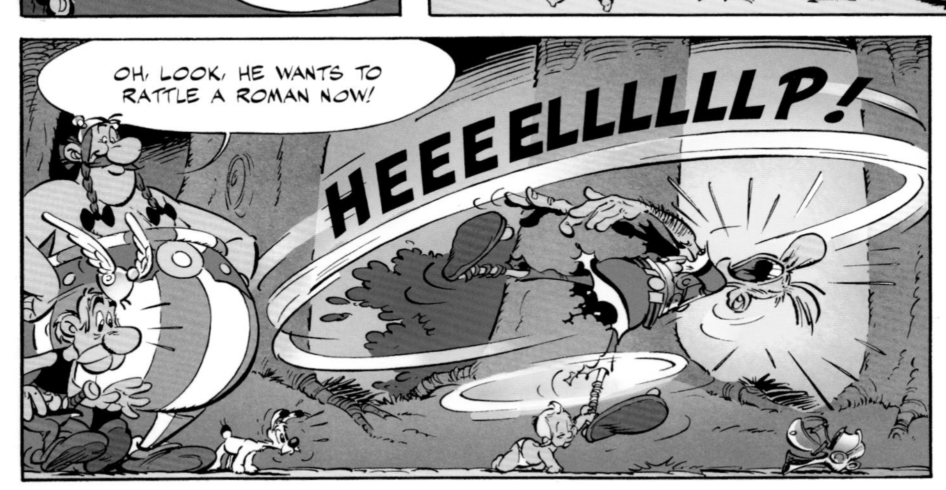
OH, LOOK, HE WANTS TO RATTLE A ROMAN NOW!
HEEEELLLLLLP!

PAF!
GOO! GOO!

YOU KNOW, WE TWO HAVE A LOT IN COMMON!
GA!

RUN FOR IT! BIG GAULS HAVE LITTLE GAULS UPON THEIR BACKS TO BITE 'EM...
OR US! AND LITTLE GAULS HAVE LESSER GAULS...
AND SO AD INFINITUM!
SHUT UP AND KEEP GOING!

ANWHILE, AT CONDATUM, IN THE
SIDENCE OF THE PREFECT OF
MORICA...
QUICK!
SEND A MESSENGER OFF
TO ROME!
DON'T BOTHER,
CACTUS!

BRUTUS!?
THAT'S RIGHT! I'VE COME
FROM ROME SPECIALLY TO
HEAR THE LATEST ABOUT
OUR LITTLE AFFAIR!

DGING BY YOUR
OVENLY APPEAR-
NCE, CONTACT
WITH THE LOCAL
ARBARIANS IS BAD
FOR YOU!
CONTACT WITH THEIR FISTS
IS! THIS INVESTIGATION
YOU WANTED MADE IS
A RISKY BUSINESS!

HAVE YOU
FOUND THE
BABY?
YES, I HAVE.
HE'S IN A LITTLE VILLAGE
ON THE NORTH COAST...
BUT GUARDED BY TWO
FIERCE GAULS WHO
FLATTENED AN ENTIRE
INFANTRY SECTION!

HMM... CAESAR'S OFTEN TOLD ME
ABOUT THAT VILLAGE OF CRAZY
BUT INDOMITABLE GAULS WHO
GET THEIR STRENGTH FROM
DRINKING MAGIC POTION!
13A

BUT I'LL HAVE THAT
ABY EVEN IF I HAVE
O PUT ALL GAUL TO
FIRE AND THE
SWORD!!!

LUCKILY, SOME WAY OFF...
COME ON, SON,
TRY YOUR LEGS
OUT!
GA!

LOOK, ASTERIX!
HE KNOWS HIS
HOME ALREADY!

?!
BANG!
?!

JUST LIKE ME AT
HIS AGE!
I WONDER IF WE'RE
SETTING THAT CHILD
A GOOD EXAMPLE?
AGA!
13B

LATER...
WELL, THE DOOR'S REPAIRED, THE BABY'S ASLEEP, AND DOGMATIX IS ON GUARD. SO LET'S GO AND DISCUSS THE SITUATION WITH CHIEF VITALSTATISTIX!
I'VE GOT TO DELIVER A MENHIR TO BUCOLIX FIRST!

MENHIRS HAVE A LONG SHELF LIFE... CAN'T IT WAIT?
NO, IT CAN'T. I ALWAY
MAKE SURE MY MENHIR
ARE SHIFTED BEFORE
'SELL BY' DATE!

SO THE ROMANS KNOW THE BABY IS HERE, AND THIS FAKE CENSUS OF THEIRS SUGGESTS THAT THEIR INTENTIONS AREN'T ENTIRELY HONOURABLE!
BUT WE STILL DON'T KNOW WHY SOMEONE CHOSE OUR VILLAGE AS THE PLACE TO LEAVE THE BABY.
I THINK I KNOW WHY!

THE BABY MUST NEE
PROTECTION FROM T
ROMANS... AND OUR
VILLAGE IS THE ONE S
PLACE WHERE ROMAN
WOULD NEVER DARE
COME!

CRAAASH!
?
?

ASTERIX, SINCE I'M GO
TO SEE BUCOLIX ANYWA
WOULD YOU LIKE ME TO P
UP ANOTHER COW FOR
THE LITTLE LAD?

OBELIX, MY BOY, I WISH TO GOODNESS YOU'D TAKE YOUR MENHIR OFF WHEN YOU COME INDOORS!
BUT, CHIEF, MENHIRS ARE HIGH FASHION INDOORS AS WELL AS OUT!

TOO HIGH
FOR MY DOO
BY HALF, YOU
IDIOT!

HE GETS FUNNY MOODS, DOES VITALSTATISTIX! IT'S NOT MY FAULT IF HIS DOOR ISN'T UP TO MY MENHIRS!

I'VE BROUGHT YOU THIS MENHIR TO PAY FOR THE HIRE OF YOUR COW, BUCOLIX!
OH, ARR! THERE BE SUMMAT OI WANTS TO ASK YOU, OBELIX... WHAT WERE YOU A-DOIN' OF WITH SHE? SHE BE PROPER COWED! SHE'VE NOBBUT TO SEE A BABBY NOW AND SHE DO BE CLIMBIN' TREES!

OOK, HOW ABOUT A GULAR MILK RUN? YOU ELIVER MILK BY THE CKET, UNPACKAGED, SAME I DELIVER MENHIRS! HERE SHALL I PUT THIS ONE?
OI'LL 'AVE IT IN THAT THERE FIELD, ALONG OF T'OTHERS!

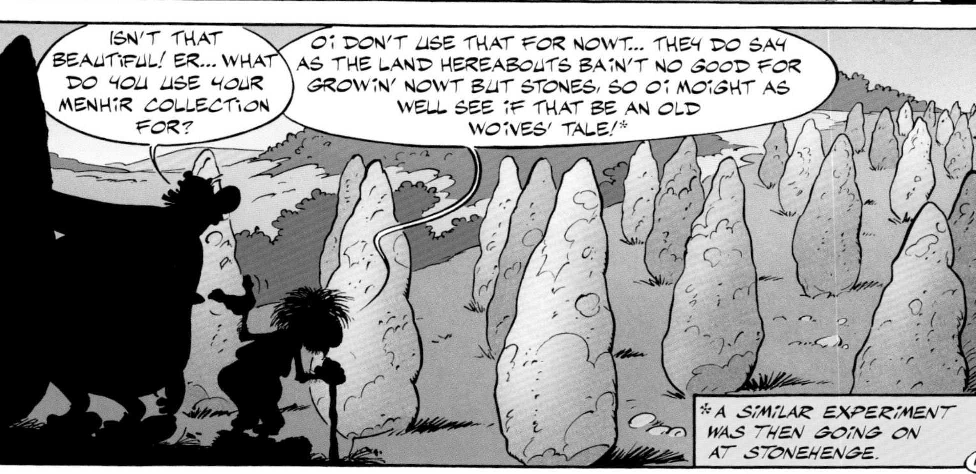

ISN'T THAT BEAUTIFUL! ER... WHAT DO YOU USE YOUR MENHIR COLLECTION FOR?
OI DON'T USE THAT FOR NOWT... THEY DO SAY AS THE LAND HEREABOUTS BAIN'T NO GOOD FOR GROWIN' NOWT BUT STONES, SO OI MOIGHT AS WELL SEE IF THAT BE AN OLD WOIVES' TALE!*
*A SIMILAR EXPERIMENT WAS THEN GOING ON AT STONEHENGE.
15A

ER...
I THINK IT MIGHT BE WISER FOR ONE OF US TO STAY AT HOME AND BABYSIT WHEN WE HAVE TO GO OUT IN FUTURE, OBELIX!
OH YES? WHICH ONE?

WELL, IN A WORD, YOU!
WORDS FAIL ME! WHY NOT YOU?

CAUSE MY TACT AND ELICACY ARE BETTER HAN YOURS WHEN IT MES TO LOOKING FOR AT BABY'S PARENTS, AND THAT'S MY LAST WORD!

OH, MY WORD!??!!
15B

DOGMATIX AND THE BABY HAVE GONE!!!

QUICK! WE MUST GO AND LOOK FOR THEM!
I CALL IT DISGRAC FUL!

NAUGHTY LITTLE BOYS LIKE THAT OUGHT TO BE KEPT INDOORS!!!
WELL, THE FACT IS, WE DID...

...I DON'T GET IT! I SIMPLY SNEEZED, I OPENED MY EYES... AND LOOK!!
?
WE'LL HAVE TO FIND HIM BEFORE GETS A FIST IN E DOOR IN THE VILLAGE!

I'VE SPOTTED HIM! HE'S AT GETAFIX'S DOOR!
WOOF!
WOOF!

COME IN!
TAP!
WOOF! GRRR! WOOF!

?
?

?
WAAAAH!
ARF! ARF! ARF!

IS SOMETHING UP, ASTERIX?
YES... THE EFFECT OF THE MAGIC POTION! IT'S WORN OFF THE BABY AT LAST. NOW FOR SOME PEACE AND QUIET!
WAAAAH!
AR
AR
AR

IN
DATUM...
SO NOW YOU KNOW THE DREADFUL SECRET OF THAT CHILD'S BIRTH, CACTUS!

AND YOU ALSO KNOW THE EQUALLY DREADFUL SECRET OF MY PLAN! IF YOU BETRAY ME, IT WILL BE THE WORSE FOR YOU!
WHAT, ME, BETRAY YOU? DO I LOOK LIKE A TRAITOR?

YES! BUT I HAVE NO CHOICE. SO IF YOU RVE ME WELL, YOU'LL GET THAT SEAT IN THE MAN SENATE YOU'VE BEEN WANTING SO LONG!
I'D SELL MY MOTHER AND FATHER TO SERVE YOU IF I HADN'T DONE THAT ALREADY, O BRUTUS, SON OF CAESAR!

ONLY ADOPTED SON OF CAESAR, AND ALL I'M ASKING YOU TO DO IS BRING ME THAT BABY!
I HAVE AN IDEA!
FLOP!

WAAAAH!
ASTERIX, SUPPOSE I GAVE HIM JUST ONE TINY DROP OF MAGIC POTION, MAYBE HE'D...

YOU'LL DO NO SUCH THING! YOU TWO HAVE CREATED ENOUGH HAVOC ALREADY!!!

LL RIGHT, ALL RIGHT, I GET IDEA! MUSTN'T TREAT THIS LACE LIKE HOME, MUST WE, DOGMATIX?
WAAAAH!
!

HEY... HE'S LEFT ME HOLDING THE BABY! OH, VERY CLEVER, MISTER OBELIX!
WAAAH!

WAAAH!
COME ON, OBELIX, DON'T BE SILLY! WHERE ARE YOU GOING?
HOME! AREN'T WE, DOGMATIX?

BUT YOU KNOW MY HOME IS YOURS!
NO, NO, IT'S YOUR HOME, AND I KNOW WHEN I'M NOT WANTED, SO LET'S FORGET IT!

LOOK, I'M SORRY. I'M RATHER EDGY AT THE MOMENT, BUT I DO NEED YOUR HELP, OBELIX!
WELL, THE BABY WAS LEFT IN YOUR CARE, WASN'T HE..?
OBELIX QUARRY

SO HE'S YOUR PROBLEM!
!
SLAM!

OH, I SEE! I GET THE IDEA! ALL YOU WANT IS AN EXCUSE TO WRIGGLE OUT OF IT! YOU KNOW WHAT YOU ARE..?
HUH!

A BIG FAT COWARD!
!!!

SAY THAT AGAIN IF YOU DARE!
YOU BET YOUR LIFE I WILL!!
NOW, NOW, CHILDREN!

AREN'T YOU ASHAMED OF YOURSELVES, QUARRELLING LIKE THAT? TWO FRIENDS... BROTHERS IN ARMS?!

SORRY, OBELIX! I WASN'T THINKING WHAT I WAS SAYING!
THAT'S ALL RIGHT... IT WAS MY FAULT! ER... LISTEN, ASTERIX...

AM I REALLY FAT..?

NO, OF COURSE NOT! JUST WELL COVERED, THAT'S ALL, YOU FATHEAD... I MEAN YOU BIG SILLY!

DRUID, WE
ST DO SOME-
G! WE'RE GAULISH
RIORS... WE'VE NO
A HOW TO BRING
P A BABY!
THE TROUBLE IS, YOU AND OBELIX ARE THE ONLY PEOPLE HE'LL HAVE NEAR HIM!

BUT NOW THE EFFECTS OF THE MAGIC POTION HAVE WORN OFF, MAYBE WE COULD HAND HIM OVER TO A NURSEMAID?
IT'S WORTH A TRY!
ANYWAY, HE'S STOPPED CRYING! THE WORST IS OVER!

OR YET TO COME! I HAVE A NASTY KIND OF FEELING...

OH, BY TOUTATIS, I THOUGHT SO! HE'S GONE AGAIN!
19A

IGHT GET INTO
UBLE... WE MUST
FIND HIM!
WE ONLY HAVE TO FOLLOW DOGMATIX!
SNIFF! SNIFF!

LUCKILY DOGMATIX IS BRIGHTER THAN THOSE STORKS!
SNIFF! SNIFF!

IT LOOKS AS IF THE BABY'S IN YOUR HOUSE, GETAFIX!
SNIFF! SNIFF!

TERIX! THE BABY'S FALLEN
INTO THE CAULDRON OF
MAGIC POTION!
OH NO! THAT REMINDS ME OF SOMETHING..!

THERE WASN'T MUCH POTION LEFT... BUT ENOUGH FOR THE EFFECTS TO LAST LONGER THIS TIME!
YOU KNOW, I REALLY TAKE TO YOU!
BURP!
AND TO THINK I ONLY FEARED THE WORST!
19B

MEANWHILE, NOT FAR FROM THE VILLAGE...
O MARCUS JUNIUS BRUTUS, SINCE WE WANT OUR HQ NEAR THE INDOMITABLE GAULS, WHY DON'T WE USE ONE OF THE FORTIFIED CAMPS SURROUNDING THEIR VILLAGE?
BECAUSE CAESAR MIGHT GET TO HEAR OF IT, AND I'M NONE TOO KEEN TO HAVE HIM ASKING ME WHAT I'M DOING HERE IN ARMORICA!

HALT! WE WILL PITCH CAMP HERE!

AND ONCE AGAIN WE ARE PRIVILEGED TO WATCH THE MANOEUVRES OF THE ROMAN ARMY. WHILE THE SAPPERS DIG A FOSSA (DITCH) AND RAISE AN AGGER (RAMPART)...

...THE WOODCUTTERS GO TO CHOP DOWN TREES...

...FOR THE CARPENTERS TO BUILD THE VALLUM (FENCE).

AT LAST THE CAMP IS READY. THE GENERAL AND HIS MEN ARE ABOUT TO ENTER IN REVIEW ORDER, THUS SYMBOLIZING THE MIGHT OF THE ROMAN ARMY, THE BEST-DISCIPLINED FIGHTING FORCE IN THE WORLD...
?

...ALTHOUGH SOMETIMES...
WHAT'S THAT?
MY TENT! I CAN'T STAN THE WAY TH OTHERS SNO IN BED!

E'S ODORIFERUS, THE LEGIONARY I MENTIONED, O BRUTUS!
HOW DID YOU KNOW WE WERE LOOKING FOR A BABY, ODORIFERUS?
I SORT OF, LIKE, HEARD THE PREFECT MENTION IT TO THE CENTURION AT AQUARIUM, O GENERAL, AND I LIKE, Y'KNOW NEARLY BROUGHT YOU THE BABY BACK!

SO WHAT STOPPED YOU?
HE DID! HE SORT OF TOOK ME FOR A RATTLE, Y'KNOW, AND THEN HE, LIKE, SWUNG ME AROUND OVER HIS HEAD, O GENERAL!

OUR MAN SEEMS TO HAVE HAD A KNOCK ON THE CAPUT*!
BUT HE'S NOT QUITE KAPUT... AND HE MAY YET BE USEFUL!
*ROMAN HEAD.

WELL, IF THIS BABY LIKES PLAYING WITH RATTLES, YOU CAN TAKE HIM SOME, ODORIFERUS! DISGUISE YOURSELF AS A GAULISH PEDLAR AND INFILTRATE THE VILLAGE OF THE INDOMITABLE GAULS! THEN YOU CAN EASILY SNATCH THE BABY AND BRING HIM BACK TO US!

IF YOU AGREE, AND SUCCEED, YOU'LL GET TO BE OPTIO!
AND IF I, LIKE, SAY NO, Y'KNOW?

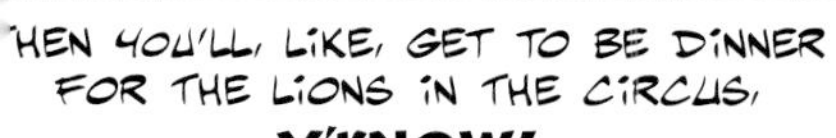
HEN YOU'LL, LIKE, GET TO BE DINNER FOR THE LIONS IN THE CIRCUS,

Y'KNOW!

LATER...
THE DISGUISE IS PERFECT... IT'S EVEN TAKEN IN THE SENTRY!
DIDN'T YOU READ THE NOTICE? NO PEDLARS OR CIRCULARS IN THIS CAMP!
POC!

ND TO THINK I, LIKE, JOINED UP BECAUSE OF THE SMART UNIFORM!

LATER STILL, JUST OUTSIDE ASTERIX'S VILLAGE...
GET OUT! NO PEDLARS OR CIRCULARS IN THIS VILLAGE!
PAF!

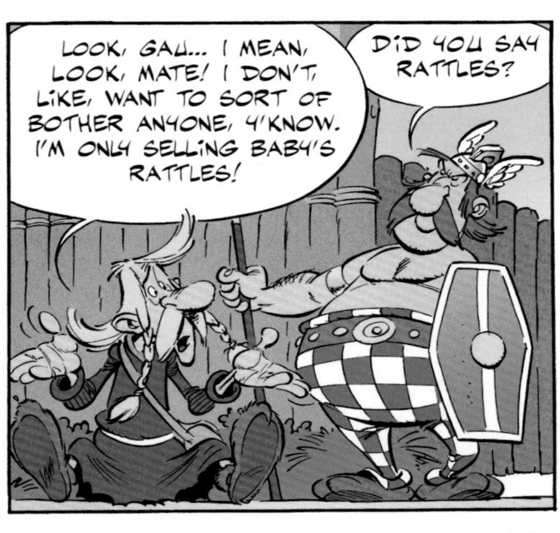
LOOK, GAU... I MEAN, LOOK, MATE! I DON'T, LIKE, WANT TO SORT OF BOTHER ANYONE, Y'KNOW. I'M ONLY SELLING BABY'S RATTLES!
DID YOU SAY RATTLES?

THAT'S DIFFERENT! GO ON IN AND SEE ASTERIX! HE'LL BE GLAD TO BUY AT LEAST ONE!

YOU'LL FIND HIS HOUSE EASILY... IT'S THE ONE WITH THE DOOR BASHED IN!

TAP! TAP!
IS THIS ASTERIX'S HOUSE?
NO, IT'S FARTHER ON!

IS THIS ASTERIX'S HOUSE?
NO, IT'S FARTHER ON!
TAP! TAP! TAP!

IS ASTERIX'S HOUSE FARTHER ON?
NO, THIS IS IT!

WHO ARE YOU AND WHAT DO YOU WANT, STRANGER?
MY NAME IS AROMATIX AND I'M, LIKE, SORT OF A PEDLAR, Y'KNOW. I WAS TOLD YOU COULD DO WITH A RATTLE!

WAAAH
IF IT'LL KEEP HIM QUIET I'LL BUY YOUR WHOLE STOCK!

WAAH
KIDDIES, LIKE, LO
MY RATTLES, Y'KNO
WATCH THIS!

WHO'D LIKE ONE OF UNCLE AROMATIX'S NICE RATTLES, THEN?
RATTLE RATTLE RATTLE
?

HELP! SAVE ME!
RATTLE RATTLE
TEEHEE! GOO! GA!
RATTLE
RATTLE
RATTLE
SO WHAT? HE JUST PREFER
THE PEDLAR OF THE RATTLES
THE RATTLES OF THE PEDL
THAT'S ALL!

PAF!

YOU KNOW, RATTLING PEDLARS ISN'T VERY NICE!
GA!
I'M TERRIBLY SORRY!
THAT'S OKAY! I SORT OF LOVE KIDDIES, Y'KNOW!

E STILL HAVE TO SOLVE THE PROBLEM. IF ONLY E COULD TAKE HIM OUT NTING BOARS WITH US... BUT HE MIGHT COME HOME AND THUMP ALL THE VILLAGE ANIMALS!

YOU MUST GET AROUND THE COUNTRYSIDE A LOT, AROMATIX. MAYBE YOU KNOW A NURSEMAID WHO'D BE BRAVE AND STRONG ENOUGH TO COME AND LOOK AFTER THIS BABY?
SURE! BUT IF, LIKE, YOU'RE SORT OF BUSY, WHY DON'T I LOOK AFTER HIM MYSELF FOR A WHILE, JUST TO HELP OUT, Y'KNOW?

YOU THINK WE OUGHT TO TAKE THE RISK, OBELIX?
IT'S THE PEDLAR WHO'D BE TAKING A RISK!
234

ELL, FINE, BUT D HE DOESN'T T OUT OF THE UT! WE'LL BE BACK QUITE SOON!
WE'RE ONLY GOING TO PICK OFF TWO OR THREE BOARS IN THE FOREST FOR SUPPER THIS EVENING!

BANG!
OUCH!
PAF!
OW!
I THINK THAT PEDLAR'S A RATTLING GOOD SORT TO AMUSE THE BABY, DON'T YOU, ASTERIX?

GA?
I WONDER IF, LIKE, THE LIONS IN THE CIRCUS MIGHT HAVE, SORT OF, BEEN A BETTER BET!

LATER...
HE'S ASLEEP AT LAST! NOW TO GET HIM BACK TO THE CAMP BEFORE HE WAKES UP!
238

GOO!
!

OH NO!!!
NOT AGAIN!!

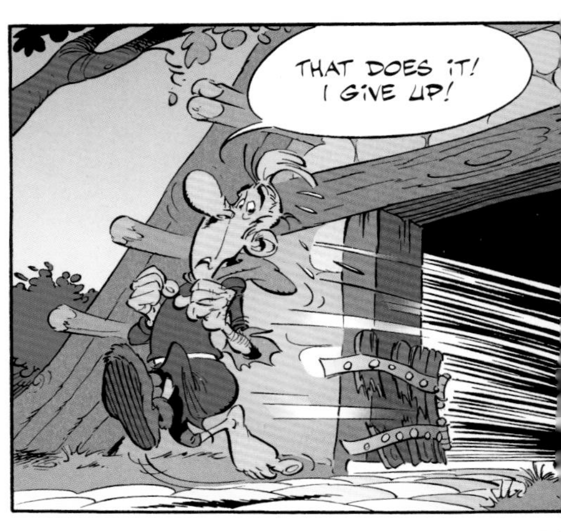
THAT DOES IT! I GIVE UP!

HELP... HE'S AFTER ME!!!

MUMMY! MUMMY!
?

HELP! HELP!

YAWN!

HALT!
WHO GOES THERE? I TOLD YOU: NO PEDLARS OR CIRCULARS...

...IN THIS CAMP!
PAF!

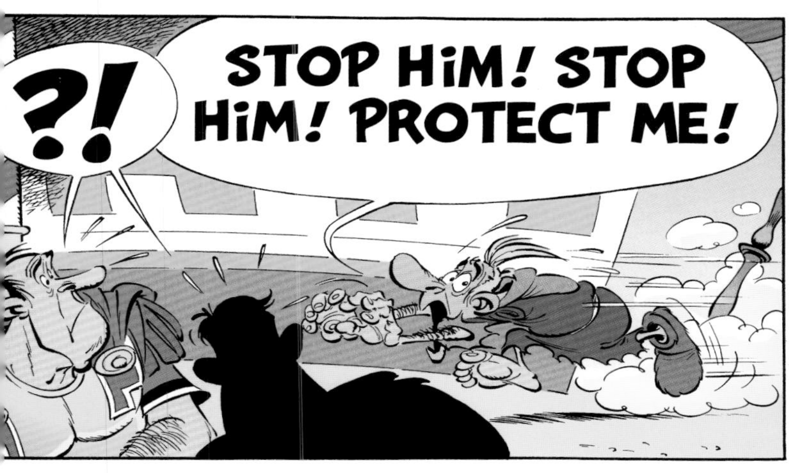
?!
STOP HIM! STOP HIM! PROTECT ME!

ODORIFERUS, COME DOWN! AND THAT'S AN ORDER!
NO! NOOOO! I'D RATHER, LIKE, GO TO THE CIRCUS!

HARDLY HAD TIME TO SPOT UR LITTLE FRIEND... BUT HE WAS AFTER THE PEDLAR, AND THE DLAR WAS IN SUCH A STATE HIS HAIR, BEARD AND MOUSTACHE HAD ALL DROPPED OUT!
!
!

QUICK, OBELIX! WE MUST FIND THAT BABY!
DOGMATIX IS ALREADY ON HIS SCENT!
SNIFF!
SNIFF!

KEEP OUR BOARS ON ICE FOR US, FOTOGENIX. WE WON'T BE LONG!
25A

AT PEDLAR WAS NO ORE A GAUL THAN A ROMAN! HE CAME O KIDNAP THE BABY!

IT'S A FUNNY THING, THE ROMANS BEING SO KEEN TO GET HOLD OF THAT CHILD!
YES! IT'S AS I ALWAYS THOUGHT.

WHAT IS?
THESE ROMANS ARE CRAZY!
TAP!
TAP!
TAP!

HERE HE IS, OBELIX! DOGMATIX HAS FOUND THE BABY!
DID YOU THINK HE WOULDN'T?
WOOF!
WOOF!

HE'S FAST ASLEEP! WE USTN'T WAKE HIM!
I THINK HE'S DIGESTING THE PEDLAR!

FOR THE LAST TIME, ODORIFERUS, COME DOWN OR I'LL CHOP THE TENT POLE DOWN INSTEAD!
PROMISE ME THAT LITTLE MONSTER ISN'T IN THE CAMP!
I KNEW THAT MAN WAS UP THE POLE!
25B

NOW, DRINK THIS PICK-ME-UP AND TELL US WHAT HAPPENED, ODORIFERUS!
I, LIKE, SORT OF WON THE GAULS' CONFIDENCE, Y'KNOW, AND THEY GAVE ME THE BABY TO LOOK AFTER...

I WAS GOING TO CARRY HIM OFF WHILE THEY WERE OUT, BUT THAT LITTLE MONSTER HAS, LIKE SUPERHUMAN STRENGTH, Y'KNOW, AND WHENEVER HE SEES ME HE SORT OF GOES INTO THE SAME ROUTINE, HE TAKES ME FOR A RATTLE AND...
HERE WE GO AGAIN!

EVEN THE GAULISH VILLAGERS ARE HAVING TROUBLE WITH HIM. ASTERIX HIMSELF ASKED IF I KNEW A NURSEMAID BRAVE AND STRONG ENOUGH TO LOOK AFTER HIM!
DID HE REALLY?

I THINK I'VE, LIKE EARNED PROMOTION TO OPTIO!
YOU? YOU'VE FAILED IN YOUR MISSION. THINK YOURSELF LUCKY NOT TO BE SERVED UP TO THE LIONS IN THE CIRCUS MAXIMUS!

I DIDN'T, LIKE, KNOW THESE PARTS BEFORE, BUT I WON'T BE SORT OF FORGETTING THE DISCOVERY OF ARMORICA IN A HURRY!

WHAT HE SAID ABOUT THE NURSEMAID GAVE ME AN IDEA! WHY DON'T WE SEND ONE TO THE VILLAGE?
BECAUSE WE HAVEN'T GOT A NURSEMAIDS THE ARMY, THA WHY!
PAF!

YES, WE HAVE... YOU!
WHAT DO YOU MEAN, ME?

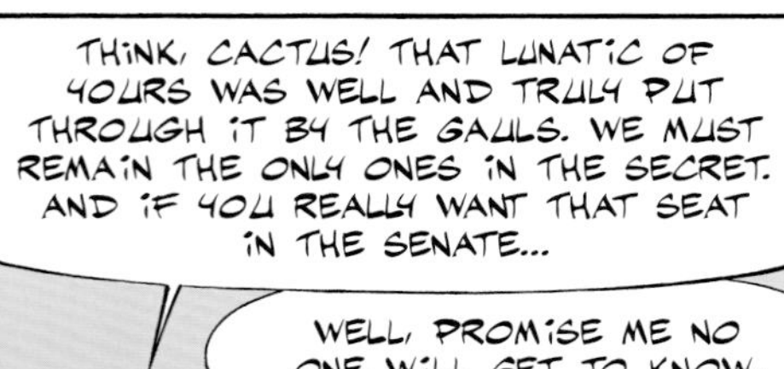
THINK, CACTUS! THAT LUNATIC OF YOURS WAS WELL AND TRULY PUT THROUGH IT BY THE GAULS. WE MUST REMAIN THE ONLY ONES IN THE SECRET. AND IF YOU REALLY WANT THAT SEAT IN THE SENATE...

WELL, PROMISE ME NO ONE WILL GET TO KNOW, ANYWAY!

LATER...
AVE, GORGEOUS! LIKE A BIT OF SLAP AND TICKLE?

SLAP!

BY ZHUPITER! THAT'SH GOING A BIT TOO FAR!
IT WORKS! EVEN THE SENTRY WAS TAKEN IN!

HULLO, GORGEOUS! LIKE A BIT OF SLAP AND TICKLE?

NO, I WOULD NOT! HOW ABOUT YOUR SISTER, THEN?

RATHER CRUDE, BUT WHAT A VOICE, BY BELENOS!

WHO ON EARTH IS THAT?
YOU CAN TELL SHE'S NOT FROM THIS VILLAGE!
SHE SHOULD WATCH HER WEIGHT!
WHAT TERRIBLE TASTE IN CLOTHES!
WHAT'S SHE AFTER HERE?
UNHYGI
ISHMO
27A

(FALSETTO) EXCUSE ME, LADIES, COULD YOU TELL ME WHERE TO FIND THE WARRIOR ASTERIX?
SHMO

HE'S REPAIRING THE DOOR OF HIS HUT, OVER THERE... YOU CAN'T MISS HIM!

A SMALL MAN WITH A YELLOW MOUSTACHE... BUT PERHAPS YOU TWO HAVE MET ALREADY?
(FALSETTO) YES... ER, I MEAN NO! THANKS!

ARE YOU THINKING WHAT I'M THINKING?
RHUBARB RHUBARB RHUBARB
BLAHBLAH BLAH
RHUBARB RHUBARB
ISHMO

(FALSETTO) ARE YOU ASTERIX?
YES. WHY?
BANG! BANG! BANG!
27B

(FALSETTO) MY NAME IS ASPIDISTRA, AND I HEARD YOU WERE LOOKING FOR A NURSE. I'M A VERY EXPERIENCED NURSEMAID!
?!
BUT YOU'RE NOT ONE OF OUR VILLAGERS... HOW DID YOU KNOW I WAS LOOKING FOR A NURSE?
(FALSETTO) OH, THESE THINGS GET AROUND THE LEGION... I MEAN THE REGION! SPECIALLY WHEN IT'S SOMETHING TO DO WITH THE BOLD AND FAMOUS WARRIOR ASTERIX!
!?
HOW ABOUT ME? DO THEY KNOW ABOUT ME IN THE REGION?
?
(FALSETTO) CAN I REALLY BE SPEAKING TO OBELIX, THE HANDSOME AND SEDUCTIVE MENHIR DELIVERY MAN?
HOWEVER DID YOU GUESS?
AND DID YOU ALSO HEAR THAT THE CHILD IN QUESTION IS... ER... RATHER A HANDFUL?
(FALSETTO) I'VE THUMP
THAT'S TO SAY, I'VE
BROUGHT UP WORSE, HA
FULS, I'M SURE!
WE CAN ALWAYS TRY. GO ON, THEN, BUT DON'T SAY I DIDN'T WARN YOU!
FUNNY... I HAVE A FEELING I'VE SEEN HER FACE SOMEWHERE BEFORE!
MAYBE SHE'S NO MORE A NURSE THAN THAT MAN WAS A PEDLAR... WHAT DO YOU THINK OF HER, OBELIX?
A WOMAN O
TASTE AND
DISCERNMEN
WOMAN OF TASTE OR NOT, WE'D BETTER WATCH OUT!
TCHAC!
I DID WARN YOU! HE'S IMPOSSIBLE!
OH, I'M NOT RATT
I GOT OFF TO
FLYING START.

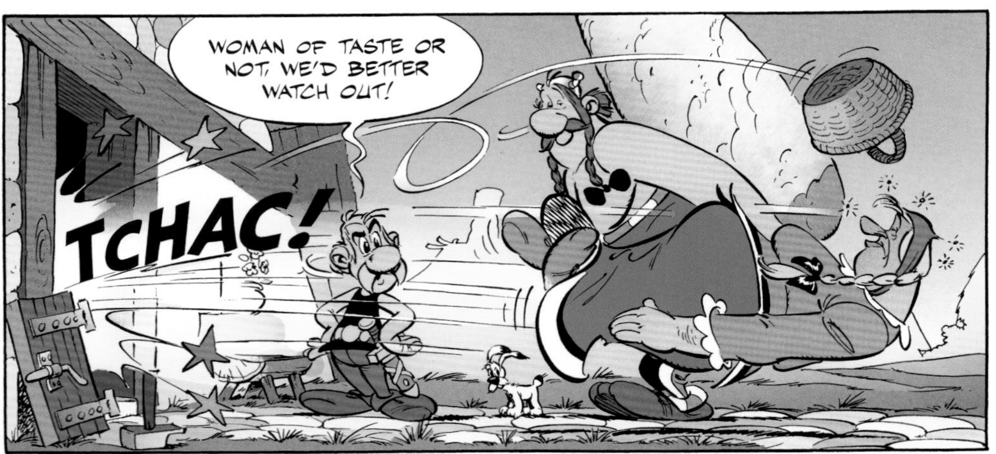

GET THE BETTER OF YOU YET, YOU CHILD!

CHLAC!
TEN TO ONE ON THE BABY!
YOU'RE ON!

S NO USE NG TO TAME AT LITTLE ONSTER, DEAR!
(NORMAL VOICE) MIND YOUR OWN BUSINESS!
I THINK THE NURSE'S VOICE IS BREAKING!

BUT I WAS ONLY GOING TO...
KEEP OUT OF THIS! GET BACK TO YOUR POTS AND PANS, WOMAN!

SPLATCH!
29a

ANCY SPEAKING TO HE CHIEF'S WIFE LIKE THAT!

YOU SEE, THE TROUBLE IS, THE BABY DRANK SOME MAGIC POTION LEFT AT THE BOTTOM OF A CAULDRON!
I'LL HAVE EARNED MY SEAT IN THE SENATE!

COME ON. I'LL TRY GETTING YOU OFF TO LESS OF A FLYING START!

OOK! THE NICEST PIDISTRA IN THE RLD! MUSTN'T HIT CE ASPIDISTRA!

WAAH!
HERE WE GO AGAIN!

GOODBYE-EE, GOODBYE-EE, WIPE THE TEAR, BABY DEAR, FROM YOUR EYE-EE...
!
29B

DON'T CRY-EE, DON'T SIGH-EE...
THE BABY SEEMS TO LIKE IT!
I CAN'T SAY I SHARE HIS TASTE!

...THERE'S A SILVER LINING IN THE SKY-EE! BONA NOX, OLD THING...
THAT'S AMAZING! ASPIDISTRA'S GOT HIM OFF TO SLEEP!

...CHEERIO, CHIN-CHIN...
WELL SHE CERTAINLY WINS THE NURSERY STAKES!
FUNNY SORT OF LULLABY, THOUGH, IF YOU ASK ME!

...NAP-POO, TOODLE-OO, GOODBYE-EE!
I CALL IT DISGRAC FUL!

WHAT'S THE MATTER, CACOFONIX?
YOU'VE BROUGHT SOMEONE IN FROM OUTSIDE TO SING! I CALL FOR EQUITY!

BUT YOU'RE NOT A NURSE, ARE YOU!
I'M A BARD, AND ONLY BARDS HAVE THE RIGHT TO SING!

NOW YOU'VE GONE AND WOKEN HIM UP! CAN'T YOU GO AND SHOUT SOMEWHERE ELSE?
MADAM, I DO NOT TAKE ORDERS FRO ANY STRANG NURSEMAIDS

AND I'LL SHOUT HERE IF I...

?

HELP! SAVE ME!
HE DOESN'T EVEN CA FOR CACOFONIX'S SPEAKING VOICE!

UNDER THE LANTERNA, BY THE STRA* GATE... MY LILIUM OF THE LANTERNA LIGHT, MY OWN LILIUM MARLENA!
I DON'T THINK SHE'S MUCH BETTER THAN CACOFONIX!
BARBARIANS! YOU'RE ALL BARBARIANS!
LOOK, YOU CAN TELL THE BABY DOESN'T LIKE YOU MUCH!
*IN: BARRACKS.

A LITTLE LATER...
HE'S DROPPED OFF AGAIN! IT'S ALL RIGHT, YOU CAN LEAVE HIM TO ME NOW!
JUST ONE THING... HOW DO YOU COME TO KNOW THESE SOLDIERS' SONGS?

A CHILDMINDER'S JOB DOESN'T PAY MUCH, SO I TOOK TO MINDING A ROMAN ARMY CANTEEN TOO. THERE ARE WAYS AND MEANS OF MOONLIGHTING, AND THAT'S MINE...

...AND THAT WAY I GOT TO BE A MINE OF INFORMATION ON THE ARMY!
OH, WON'T I JUST HAVE EARNED MY SEAT IN THE SENATE!

WAAAH!
WELL, YOU'RE NEEDED AS A CHILDMINDER NOW!
31A

OH, OH, OH, IT'S A LOVELY BELLUM...
COME ON, OBELIX! LET'S FIND SOMEWHERE QUIETER!

OH, GOOD WORK, VITALSTATISTIX! MARVELLOUS, I CALL IT!
WHAT? WHAT HAVE I GONE AND DONE NOW?

YOU'RE CHIEF OF THIS VILLAGE... YOU LET A WOMAN FROM OUTSIDE COME AND LIVE UNDER A BACHELOR'S ROOF? OH, THAT'S GREAT!
BUT PEDIMENTA DEAR, SHE'S ONLY A NURSE FOR THE BABY!

EXACTLY! SUCH PROMISCUITY! SHOCKING!

I'M NOT ENJOYING THIS ADVENTURE VERY MUCH, OBELIX!
OH, IT'LL BE ALL RIGHT! IT'S SURE TO END WITH A BANQUET UNDER THE STARRY SKY, SAME AS USUAL!
31B

I'D LIKE A PRIVATE WORD WITH YOU, ASTERIX!
!

ABOUT THAT NURSE LIVING UNDER YOUR ROOF.. TONGUES A BEGINNING TO WAG! COULD YOU AND STAY SOMEWHERE ELSE FO THE TIME BEING?
I COULDN'T CARE LESS ABOUT VILLA GOSSIP, BUT I'LL AS YOU SUGGEST VITALSTATISTIX! JU TO OBLIGE YOU!

WHAT ARE YOU DOING?
MOVING OUT! IF YOU NEED ME, I'LL BE AT OBELIX'S PLACE!

HO, HO! THE FOOL'S LEFT THE COAST CLEAR FOR ME! NOW I CAN EASILY MAKE OFF WITH THE BABY AT DEAD OF NIGHT.

WAA
MADEMOISELLE FROM ARMORICA, PARLEY-VOO...
TO BE HONEST, I'LL BE RATHER GLAD TO STAY WITH OBELIX JUST NOW!

AND THAT NIGHT...
NOW'S MY MOMENT! EVERYONE'S ASLEEP, INCLUDING HIM!

WAAAH!

WAAH!
IT WAS SOLSTICE DA IN THE CULINA*...
*ROMAN ARMY COOKHOUSE

AND A VERY UNHAPPY SOLSTICE TO YOU TOO!
ONLY BARDS HAVE THE RIGHT TO SING!
CALL THAT SINGING?
WILL SOME-BODY MAKE THAT WOMAN SHUT UP?
PUT A SOCK IN IT, WILL YOU?
FOILED!
THERE, THERE, PEDIMENTA!
COCK-A-DOODLE-D

MORNING..
OH, I WILL HAVE EARNED THAT SEAT IN THE SENATE, AND NO MISTAKE!

BUT FOR THE EFFECTS OF THAT WRETCHED POTION, I'D TUCK HIM UNDER MY ARM AND MAKE OFF WITH HIM NOW!
BURP!
PAT! PAT! PAT!

COME TO THINK OF IT, HOW DO I KNOW THE POTION'S STILL WORKING ON YOU, EH?
GA?

GA!
CLOCK!

33A

ERYTHING OKAY?
SORT OF... ARE THE EFFECTS OF THAT MAGIC POTION GOING TO LAST MUCH LONGER?

THAT DEPENDS! JUDGING BY OBELIX, THEY COULD LAST FOR EVER!

AND SO, A LITTLE LATER...
WELL, I'M NOT GOING TO STICK AROUND IN THIS ROTTEN VILLAGE FOR EVER, WEARING THESE ROTTEN CLOTHES AND PLAYING THIS ROTTEN PART!

TOO BAD! I'LL RISK IT!

WHERE ARE YOU GOING, GORGEOUS?
ER... I'M GOING INTO THE FOREST TO PICK MUSHROOMS!

?
WAAAH!
33B

PACK UP YOUR TROUBLES IN YOUR OLD SARCINA*, AND SMILE, SMILE, SMILE...
?!
*LATIN: KIT-BAG.

SO NOW WE'RE OUT OF SIGHT OF THE VILLAGE...

...I'LL MAKE STRAIGHT FOR THE CAMP!

WHERE ARE YOU GOING, OBELIX?
I'M DELIVERING A MENHIR TO BUCOLIX. THAT BABY HAS A GOOD APPETITE... HE'S COSTING US MANY A MENHIR!

I'LL COME WITH YOU!

IF YOU'RE LOOKING FOR THE BABY AND HIS NURSE, THEY'VE GONE INTO THE FOREST TO PICK MUSHROOMS!
?!

QUICK, OBELIX! I'VE GOT A NASTY FEELING...
KEEP MY MENHIR ON ICE, FOTOGENIX! WE SHAN'T BE VERY LONG!
SNIFF! SNIFF!

PHEW! THAT'S A WEIGHT OFF MY MIND!

GA!
MY MIND?

THROWING YOUR WEIGHT AROUND, EH? WAIT TILL I CATCH YOU, YOU !

!
REECH!
SCREEEECH

HELP! HELP!
SAVE ME!

CHOC!

NOOOO!
DON'T TOUCH ME!
LEAVE ME ALONE!!!
GA!
35A

MUMM

A LITTLE LATER..
OH, LOOK! ISN'T HE SWEET? HE'S GONE TO SLEEP UNDER A TREE AGAIN!
WOOF! WOOF! WOOF!

THIS PROVES
PIDISTRA'S STORY OF
NLIGHTING IN AN ARMY
CANTEEN WAS ALL
ONSHINE! WE'VE BEEN
FOOLED!

WHY DON'T WE FIND OUT WHO SHE REALLY WAS? I'D LOVE TO INVESTIGATE A ROMAN CAMP AGAIN!
WE CAN'T PUT THE BABY AT RISK. THE ROMANS WILL BE SURE TO THINK SOMETHING ELSE UP.. BUT THIS TIME, BY TOUTATIS, WE'LL BE READY FOR THEM!
35B

HELP! HELP! SAVE ME!

YESH, BY ZHUPITER! COME TO MY...

...ARMS!
SPLATCH!

DON'T BE RIDICULOUS, CACTUS! I ORDER YOU TO COME DOWN!
PROMISE ME HE ISN'T IN THE CAMP!

TOO BAD! SO I WON'T GET TO BE SENATOR... BUT DON'T ANYONE EVER MENTION THAT MONSTER TO ME AGAIN!
NOW, NOW! WE'VE LO A BATTLE, WE HAVEN LOST THE WAR!

I TOLD YOU I'D PUT ALL GAUL TO FIRE AND THE SWORD IF NECESSARY...
SO NOW LET'S LIGHT THE FIRE!!

AND AT DUSK...
FANCY MAKING US HAUL THESE ROMAN RELICS UP, JUST TO SHOOT OFF A LOT OF FIERY ARROWS!
YES, IT'S A FLAMING NUISANCE!

ARE YOU REALLY GOING TO PUT ALL GAUL TO FIRE AND THE SWORD, BRUTUS?
WELL, THE VILLAGE OF THOSE INDOMITABLE GAULS WILL DO! I'M TOLD THE THATCH ON GAULISH HUTS BURNS FAST AND WELL.

THIS TIME THE ROMANS HAVE TURNED OUT MORE CUNNING AND PERSISTENT THAN USUAL!
SO WE MUST TAKE MORE CARE THAN USUAL!
AND GOSSIP LESS, TOO!
YOU WOULD KEE A-HOLD OF N AND YOU FO SOMETHIN WORSE!

NIGHT, SEVERAL
PASSUUM*
M THE VILLAGE...
GET IT, CACTUS? I'M LEAVING YOU IN COMMAND! WHEN I GIVE THE SIGNAL, OPEN FIRE!
LLE PASSUS = 1 ROMAN MILE.

A FIERY ARROW! THE SIGNAL!

ARE YOU READY..?

CHAC!
FIRE!

THE ROMANS ARE ATTACKING!!!
FIRE!
THE VILLAGE IS BURNING!
COCK-A-DOODLE-DO!

IMPEDIMENTA, YOU TAKE THE WOMEN AND CHILDREN DOWN TO THE BEACH WHILE WE DEAL WITH THE ROMANS!
I'LL LEAVE HIM IN YOUR CARE! I'M SURE HE'LL BE GOOD!

EVERYBODY LINE UP IN SILENCE, AND DON'T PANIC!

NO?
NO!
GLUG! GLUG! GLUG!
IT SEEMS TO TASTE RATHER FUNNY THIS TIME!
I EXPECT IT GOT A BIT BURNT IN THE HEAT OF THE MOMENT.

THE ROMANS ARE PLAYING WI FIRE... NOW LET SHOW THEM WHA WE CAN COOK
CHARG

CHARGE!
INVESTIGATORS FIRST! ISN'T THAT RIGHT, ASTERIX?

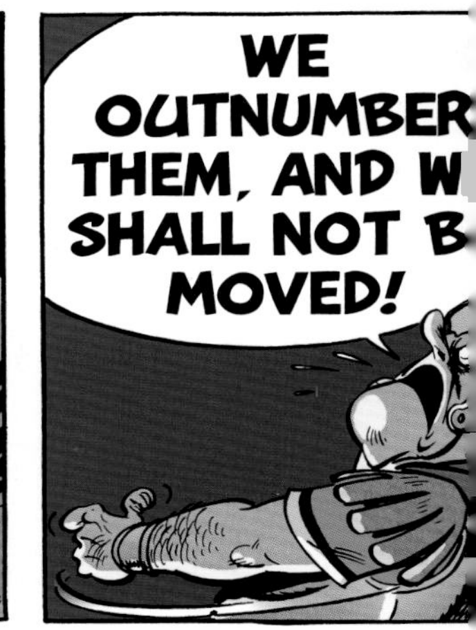
WE OUTNUMBER THEM, AND W SHALL NOT B MOVED!

CRAAAAAAASH!

...ANWHILE...
WE'LL BE
...UITE SAFE
HERE!

HAND ME THAT BABY, MY GOOD WOMAN!
?!

COME AND GET HIM IF YOU DARE!
YOU DON'T SCARE US, ROMAN! WE'VE HAD OUR PORTION OF MAGIC POTION!
WE HAVE? I DIDN'T GET ANY!
SSH! SHUT UP!
39 A

...OH NO! HE'S GETTING AWAY!

LEAVE IT TO HIM, DEAR! THAT ROMAN'S IN FOR A SURPRISE!

SO THIS IS THE TERRIBLE LITTLE MONSTER?
BY BELISAMA! THE EFFECTS OF THE POTION HAVE WORN OFF!
WAAAH!

WAAH!
OUT TO THE SHIP... FAST!

AND SOON...
DO YOU SWEAR THERE'S NO RISK OF THOSE CRAZY GAULS TURNING UP?
THEY'RE FAR TOO BUSY JUST NOW!
39 B

SO THEY ARE... AND AT DAWN...
COCK-A...
COUGH-A... COUGH!

LOOK, ASTERIX! I'VE MET THE PEDLAR AGAIN!
AND I'VE MET THE NURSE!
IT'S A GOOD THING WE OUTNUMBER THEM, OR WE MIGHT HAVE BEEN MOVED!
PAF! PAF! PAF! PAF!

NOW, TELL ME WHAT REALLY BROUGHT YOU HERE, OR YOU'LL HAVE A FEW TROUBLES OF YOUR OWN TO PACK UP IN YOUR OLD SARCINA!
MERCY! I WAS ONLY OBEYING THE ORDERS OF CAESAR'S SON, BRUTUS!

AND WHERE IS BRUTUS?
ON THE BEACH! HE KNEW YOU'D SEND THE BABY TO SAFETY THERE!

QUICK, OBELIX! FOLLOW ME!
QUICK, DOGMATIX! FOLLOW US!
WOOF! WOOF!

WHERE'S THE BABY?
ASTERIX, I HAVE FAILED YOU! A ROMAN SNATCHED HIM AND TOOK HIM ON BOARD A PIRATE SHIP!

I CAN STILL SEE IT ON THE HORIZON!
DO YOU THINK YOU COULD SWIM OUT THAT FAR?

YOU REALLY DO ASK STUPID QUESTIONS SOMETIMES, ASTERIX!

WELL, OF COURSE I CAN!

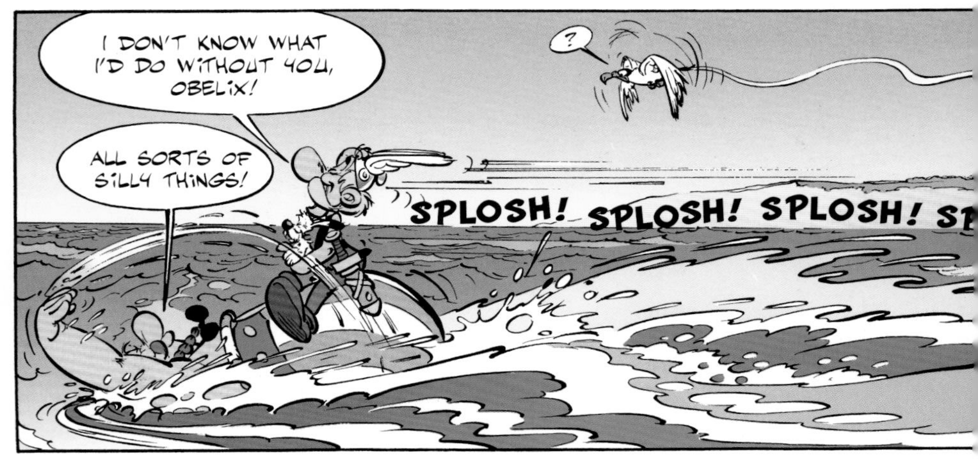

I DON'T KNOW WHAT I'D DO WITHOUT YOU, OBELIX!
ALL SORTS OF SILLY THINGS!
?
SPLOSH! SPLOSH! SPLOSH!

WE'VE FIXED
E PRICE, THEN, ROMAN?
YES, BUT YOU DON'T GET PAID UNTIL WE DIS-EMBARK AT BRIVATES PORTUS*.
*BREST.

THAT'S OKAY! I'VE A WIFE IN EVERY PORTUS... SO THAT SUITS MY BRIVATE LIFE!

THE LAD MUST BE WORTH A LOT!
EVEN MORE THAN YOU THINK!

SHIVER ME TIMBERS...
F HE'S THAT VALUABLE,
'VE A GOOD MIND TO
EEP HIM FOR MYSELF!

TWO SWIMMERS ON OUR WAVE-LENGTH!
?

TWO SWIMMERS? WHO ARE THEY?

GAULS! THEY'RE MAKING WAVES! WE'RE IN DEEP WATER!
!
41 A

URELY YOU'RE
T ABANDONING
SHIP JUST
CAUSE OF TWO
GAULS?
YOU DON'T KNOW US, YOU NEVER SET EYES ON US, AND NOW WE'RE QUITS, ROMAN!

YOOHOO!

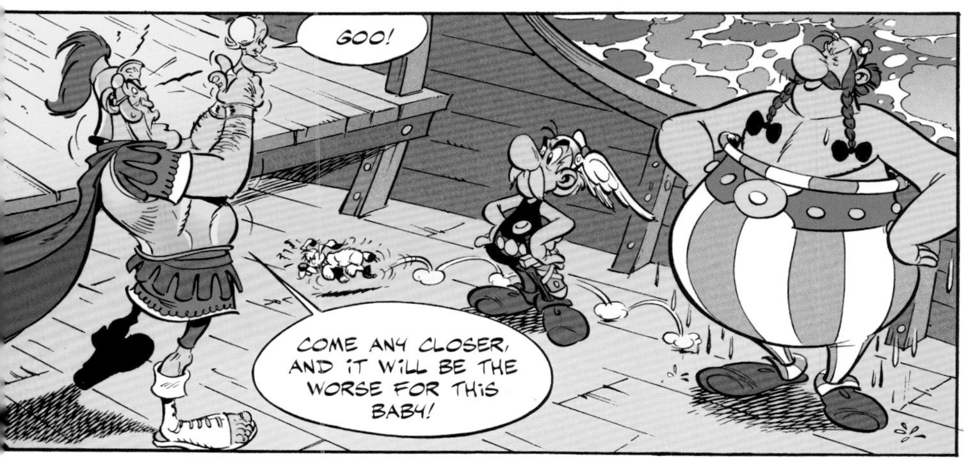
GOO!
COME ANY CLOSER, AND IT WILL BE THE WORSE FOR THIS BABY!

OUCH!
OW!
GRRRRR!
41 B

AND WE DIDN'T EVEN SEE THE PIRATES! DO THEY KNOW WHAT'S UP?
OH, I'M SURE THEY'RE IN THE SWIM!

WE'RE TWO DAYS' SWIM FROM BRIVATES PORTUS... IT'LL BE A LONG CRAWL! TRY DOING THE BREST-STROKE! THOSE GAULS ARE SICKENING!
SIC! AD NAUSEAM!
I'M FEELING A BIT SEASIC (SIC) MYSELF!

SOON AFTERWARDS...
I KNEW THEY'D BRING THE BABY BACK ALL RIGHT!
HURRAY FOR ASTERIX!
HURRAY FOR OBELIX!
HURRAY FOR DOGMATIX!

HAVE YOU DISCOVERED THE SECRET OF THE CHILD'S BIRTH, ASTERIX?
NOT YET, BUT I HAVE THE KEY TO THE MYSTERY!
AND JUST WHAT IS GOING ON HERE?

?!!
CAESAR!

YES, BRUTUS! I HAVE COME STRAIGHT FROM UPPER GERMANIA, WHERE MY SPIES TOLD ME WHAT YOU WERE UP TO!

DECIMATING MY LEGIONS JUST TO GET HOLD OF A BABY! AND WHO IS THIS BABY? WELL, OUT WITH IT!
JUST WHAT I WAS GOING TO ASK HIM MYSELF, JULIUS, OLD CHAP!

THAT BABY, O CAESAR, I YOUR SON!!

CLEOPATRA!
?!
AMAZING! WHAT A SIGHT!
AND WHAT A NOSE!

SON? CAESARION? T I THOUGHT YOU RE BOTH SAFE IN PALACE IN ROME!
DID YOU SAY SAFE?

AFTER YOU LEFT, THE VILLAINOUS BRUTUS MADE SEVERAL ATTEMPTS TO DO AWAY WITH CAESARION, HOPING TO BECOME SOLE HEIR TO YOUR PROPERTY AND YOUR FORTUNE!

SO I DECIDED TO SEND OUR SON AWAY TO THE ONE PLACE WHERE I COULD BE SURE HE WOULD BE SAFE: THE VILLAGE OF INDOMITABLE GAULS WHICH STILL HOLDS OUT AGAINST THE INVADERS!
ALL RIGHT, I KNOW!

ET TU, BRUTE?* U WILL LEAVE IMMEDIATELY FOR UPPER GERMANIA! T HAS A NICE BRACING ATE, AND THE BARBARIANS THERE WILL TEACH YOU MANNERS!
*YOU TOO, BRUTUS? CAESAR SOMETIMES REPEATED HIMSELF.

FORGIVE ME FOR TAKING ADVANTAGE OF YOU, ASTERIX!
OH, THAT'S ALL RIGHT! I'M HONOURED BY YOUR FAITH IN ME, QUEEN CLEOPATRA!

THE... THE BABY'S DISAPPEARED!

WOOF! WOOF!
HE'S GONE TO SLEEP UNDER A TREE AGAIN!
HE LIKES TREES, SAME AS DOGMATIX! IT'S A GOOD SIGN!
THEN I'LL HAVE SOLID GOLD TREES MADE FOR HIM!
O QUEEN CLEOPATRA, AND YOU TOO, CAESAR, WE'RE SORRY THAT WE CAN'T INVITE YOU TO CELEBRATE THIS HAPPY EVENT IN OUR VILLAGE, BUT IT'S BURNT TO ASHES!
BUT THIS IS THE END! SO WHAT ABOUT THE BANQUET?
I PROMISE YOU MY ENGINEERING CORPS WILL REBUILD YOUR VILLAGE!
AND I'LL HOLD A BANQUET FOR YOU ON BOARD GALLEY! IT'S THE LEAST I CA DO!
SO THERE IS A BANQUET AFTER ALL, IF NOT QUITE THE SORT OBELIX EXPECTS. IT IS HELD UNDER THE SUNNY SKY OF ARMORICA, ON BOARD QUEEN CLEOPATRA'S SUMPTUOUS GALLEY. EVERYTHING ELSE IS THE SAME AS USUAL, INCLUDING THE ROAST BOAR, AND JULIUS CAESAR HIMSELF JOINS THE PARTY. FOR IS HE NOT THE FATHER OF THE YOUNG HERO WHO LIES THERE SOUND ASLEEP, UNAWARE THAT ONE DAY, UNDER THE NAME OF PTOLEMY XVI, HE WILL RULE EGYPT?
...SO WHEN THE BEES HAVE COLLECTED THEIR POLLEN THE PRETTY FLOWERS ALL GET MARRIED, SEE?
AND HOW ABOUT THE STORKS? SCRUNCH! WHERE DO THE STORKS COME INTO IT?
SCRUNCH! SCRUNCH!
THE END